WARRIORS OF OLD JAPAN

Published in the same series:

Frederick Hadland, *Myths and Legends of Japan*
Lafcadio Hearn, *In Ghostly Japan*
Lafcadio Hearn, *Kwaidan*
Algernon Bertram Mitford, *Tales of Old Japan*
Eiko Ozaki, *Japanese Fairy Tales I, II*
Frank Rinder, *Old-World Japan*

TOYO CLASSICS

Warriors of Old Japan

The Illustrated Editions of Japan's Great Classics

EIKO OZAKI

First edition, 2017

Published by TOYO Press

Copyright © 2017 TOYO Press

ISBN 978-94-92722-00-3

CONTENTS

Minamoto Monjumaru Yorimitsu — 1

Minamoto Sanmi Yorimasa — 33

Minamoto Hachirō Tametomo — 53

Minamoto Ushiwakamaru Yoshitsune — 72

Musashibō Oniwaka Benkei — 96

Hōjō Saimyōji Tokiyori — 120

Glossary — 133

MINAMOTO YORIMITSU

The Giant of Oeyama

Long, long ago in Old Japan, in the reign of the Emperor Ichijō, the sixty-sixth emperor, there lived a very brave general called Minamoto no Yorimitsu. Minamoto was the name of the powerful clan to which he belonged, and Yorimitsu was his own name.

In those times it was the custom for generals to keep as a body-guard four picked warriors renowned for their daring spirit, their great strength, and their skill in wielding the sword. These four braves were called the Shitennō, or the Four Kings of Heaven, and they participated in all the exploits and martial expeditions of their chieftain, and vied with one another in excelling in bravery and dexterity.

Minamoto no Yorimitsu was no exception to the general rule of those ancient leaders of Japan, and he had under him Usui Sadamitsu, Sakata Kintoki, Urabe Suetake, and Watanabe Tsuna (the clan or surname comes first in Japan). Search the wide world from north to south and from east to west, and no braver warriors than the Shitennō of Minamoto no Yorimitsu could you find. Each one of the four was said to be a match single-handed for a thousand men. They lived for adventure, and their delight was in war.

Now it happened about this time that Kyoto, the capital, was ringing with the stories of the doings of a frightful giant who lived in the caves of a high mountain called Mount Oe, in the province of Tamba. This giant or demon's name was Shutendōji. To look upon the creature was a horrible thing, and

1

those who once caught sight of him never forgot the sight to their dying day. He sometimes took the form of a human being, and leaving his den would steal into the capital and haunt the streets and carry off precious sons and beloved daughters of the Kyoto homes. Having seized these treasures and flowers of the people, he would drag them to his castle in the caves of Mount Oe, and there he would make them work and wait upon him till he was ready to devour them, then he would tear them limb from limb.

For a long time the flower of the youth of the capital had been kidnapped in this way, and many homes had been made desolate. For a long, long time no one had the least idea of what happened to the sons and daughters thus stolen. But at the period when this story begins, the dreadful news of the cannibal Shutendōji and his mountain den began to be voiced abroad.

Now at court there was an official, Kimitaka by name, who was delighted to have a beautiful daughter. She was his only child, and upon her he and his wife doted. One day the darling of the family disappeared, and no trace whatsoever of the beautiful girl could be found. The household was plunged into the deepest grief and misery. The mother at last determined to consult a soothsayer, and, bidding an attendant follow her, she went to the house of a famous fortune-teller and diviner, who revealed to her that her daughter had been stolen away by the giant of Mount Oe. The mother hastened home terror-stricken, and the father, when he was told the terrible news, was dumb with grief. He gave up going on duty at the palace, for he was so broken-hearted that he could do nothing but weep night and day over the loss of his only daughter. To lose her was bad enough, but the thought of the horrible hands into which she had fallen was unendurable, and all who loved the poor child, even her own father, were powerless to save her. Oh! the bitter, bitter grief!

At last the emperor heard of the sorrow that had overtaken Kimitaka. His wrath was great to think that the hateful giant had dared to enter the precincts of the sacred capital without permission, and had dared to steal away his subjects in this manner. And in his royal indignation he sprang to his feet and threw down his tasselled fan and cried aloud: "Is there no one in my domains who will punish this giant and destroy him utterly, and avenge the wrongs he has done my people and this city, and so set my heart at ease?"

源頼光

Then the emperor called his council together, and put the matter before them and asked them what it were best to do, for the city must at all costs be rid of this terrible scourge.

"How dare he haunt my dominions and lay hands on my people in the very precincts of my palace?" cried the distressed emperor.

Then the ministers respectfully answered the emperor and said: "There are numbers of brave warriors in Your Majesty's realm, but there are none so able to do your bidding as Minamoto no Yorimitsu. We would humbly advise our August Emperor, the Son of Heaven, to send for the warrior and command him to slay the giant. Our poor counsel may not find favor in the Son of Heaven's sight, but at the present moment we can think of nothing else to suggest!"

This advice pleased the Emperor Ichijō, and he answered that he had often heard of Yorimitsu as a valiant warrior and true, who knew not what fear was, and he had no doubt that, as his ministers said, he was just the man for the adventure. And so the emperor summoned Yorimitsu to the palace at once.

The warrior, on receiving the royal and unexpected summons, hastened to the palace, wondering what it could mean. When he was told what was wanted of him, he prostrated himself before the throne in humble acquiescence to the royal command. Indeed Yorimitsu was very glad at the thought of the adventure in store for him, for they had been quiet some time in Kyoto, and he and his braves had chafed at the enforced idleness.

The more he realized the awful difficulty of his task, the higher his courage and his spirits rose to face it and the more he determined to do it or die in the attempt.

He went home and thought out a plan of action.

As the enemy was no human being, but a formidable giant, he thought that the wisest course would be to resort to stratagem instead of an open encounter, so he decided to take with him a few of his most trusted men rather than a great number of warriors. He then called together his four braves, Kintoki, Sadamitsu, Suetake, and Tsuna, and besides these another warrior, by the name of Hirai Yasumasa, nicknamed Hitori, which meant, as applied to him, "the only warrior."

Yorimitsu told them of the expedition, and explained that, as the giant was no common foe, he thought it wise that they should go to his mountain in disguise. In this way they would the more likely and the more easily overcome the giant. They all agreed to what their chief said and set about making their preparations with great joy. They polished up their armour and sharpened their long swords and tried on their helmets, rejoicing in the prospect of the action confronting them. Before starting on this dangerous enterprise, they thought it wise to seek the protection and blessing of the gods, so Yorimitsu and Yasumasa went to pray for help at the temple of Hachiman, the God of War, at Mount Otoko, while Tsuna and Kintoki went to the Sumiyoshi shrine of the Goddess of Mercy, and Sadamitsu and Suetake to the temple of Gongen at Kumano. At each shrine the six warriors offered up the same prayer for divine help and strength. And on bended knees and with hands laid palm to palm they besought the gods to grant them success in their expedition and a safe return to the capital.

Then the brave band disguised themselves as mountain priests. They wore priests' caps and sacerdotal garments and stoles. They hid their armour and their helmets and their weapons in the knapsacks they carried on their backs. In their right hands they carried a pilgrim's staff, and in their left a rosary, and they wore rough straw sandals on their feet. No one meeting these dignified, solemn-looking priests would have thought that they were on the way to attack the giant of Mount Oe, and no one would have dreamt that the leader of the band was the warrior Yorimitsu, who for courage and strength had not his peer in the whole of the island empire.

In this way Yorimitsu and his men travelled across the country till at last they reached the province of Tamba and came to the foot of the mountain of Oe. Now as the giant had chosen Mount Oe as his place of abode, you can imagine how difficult of access it was! Yorimitsu and his men had often travelled in mountainous districts, but they had never experienced anything like the steepness of Mount Oe. It was indescribable. Great rocks obstructed the way, and the branches of the trees were so thickly interlaced overhead that the light of day could not penetrate through the foliage even at midday, and the shadows were so black that the warriors would have been glad of lanterns. Sometimes the path led them over precipices where they could

hear the water rushing along the deep ravines beneath. So deep were these chasms that as Yorimitsu and his men passed them they were overcome with giddiness. For the first time they realized now the dangers and difficulties of the task they had undertaken, and they were somewhat disheartened. At times they rested themselves on the roots of trees to gain breath, sometimes they stopped to quench their thirst at some trickling spring, catching the water up in their hands. They did not allow themselves to be discouraged long, but pushed their way deeper and deeper into the mountain, encouraging each other with brave words of cheer when they felt their spirits flagging. But the thought sometimes crossed their minds, though they one and all kept it to themselves, "What if Shutendōji, or some of his demons, should be lurking behind any of the rocks or cliffs?"

Suddenly from behind a rock three old men appeared. Now Yorimitsu, who was as wise as he was brave, and who at that very moment had been thinking of what he should do were they to encounter the giant unexpectedly, thought that sure enough here were some of the goblins, who had heard of his approach. They had simply disguised themselves as these venerable old men so as to deceive him and his men! But he was not to be outwitted by any such prank. He made signs with his eyes to the men behind him to be on their guard, and they in obedience to his gesture put themselves in attitudes of defense.

The three old men saw at once the mistake Yorimitsu had made, for they smiled at him and then drawing nearer, they bowed before him, and the foremost one said: "Do not be afraid of us; we are not the goblins of this mountain. I am from the province of Settsu. My friend is from Kii, and the third lives near the capital. We have all been bereft of our beloved wives and daughters by Shutendōji the giant. Because of our great age we can do nothing to help them, though our sorrow for their loss, instead of growing less, grows greater day by day. We have heard of your coming, and we have awaited you here, so that we might ask you to help us in our distress. It is a great favor we ask, but we entreat you if you encounter Shutendōji to show him no mercy, but to slay him and so avenge the wrongs of our wives and children and many others who have been torn away from their homes in the Flower Capital."

"Now that you have told me so much," Yorimitsu answered, "I need not reserve the truth from you." And he went on to tell them of the order he had received from the emperor to destroy Shutendōji and his den, and the warrior did his best to comfort the old men and to assure them that he would do all in his power to restore their kidnapped wives and daughters.

Then the old men expressed great joy. Their faces beamed like the sun as they thanked Yorimitsu warmly for his kind sympathy, and they presented him with a jar of *saké*, saying as they bowed low: "As a token of our gratitude we wish to present you with this magic wine. It is called Shimben Kidoku-Shu.' The name means, 'a cordial for men but a poison to giants.' Therefore if a giant drinks of this wine, all his strength will go from him, and he will be as one paralyzed. Before you attack Shutendōji, give him to drink of this wine, and for the rest you will find no difficulty."

And with these words the venerable spokesman handed the warrior a small white stone jar containing the wine. As soon as Yorimitsu had taken the jar into his hands, a radiance like that of sunlight suddenly shone round the old men, and they vanished upwards from sight till their shining figures were lost in the clouds.

The three old men vanish from sight

The warriors were struck with astonishment. They gazed upwards as if stupefied. But Yorimitsu was the first to recover from his surprise. He clapped his hands and laughed as he said: "Be not afraid at what you have seen! Be sure that the three who thus appeared to us are none other than the gods of the shrines we visited before starting on this perilous enterprise. The old man who said he was from Settsu must have been the deity of Sumiyoshi, the one from the province of Kii was the divinity of Kumano, and the one from the capital the god Hachiman of Mount Otoko. This is a most propitious sign. The three deities have taken us under their special protection. This *saké* is their gift, and it will surely be of magic power in helping us to overcome the demons. We must, therefore, render thanks to Heaven for the protection vouchsafed to us."

Then Yorimitsu and his five warriors knelt down on the mountain pass and bowed themselves to the ground and prayed for some minutes in silence, overcome with awe at the thought that the three gods whose aid they had invoked had visited them. Yorimitsu sprang to his feet and lifted the jar of *saké* reverently above his head, then he placed it with his armour and weapons in the box he carried on his back. Having done this, they all proceeded on their way, but oh! how safe and confident they now felt. Yorimitsu

Yorimitsu and his men launch their assault on Mount Oe

The warriors meet the
damsel at the stream

with his magic wine felt more than a match for any demon now. There is a proverb which says, "A giant with an iron rod," which means strength added to strength, and this was fully illustrated in the case of Yorimitsu. The giant Shutendōji was now to be pitied; it would surely go hard with him!

As they sped on their way they came to a mountain stream, and here they found a damsel washing a blood-stained garment, and as she washed and beat the garment against the current, they saw that she often had to stop and wipe the tears away with her sleeve, for she was weeping bitterly. Yorimitsu's heart was stirred with pity at her distress, and he went up to her and said: "This is a haunted mountain. How is it that I find a damsel such as you here?"

The princess (for such she was) looked up in his face wonderingly and said: "It is indeed true that this is a haunted mountain, and hitherto inaccessible to mortals. How is it that you have managed to get here?" and she looked from Yorimitsu to his men.

Then Yorimitsu said: "I will tell you the truth quite frankly. The emperor has commanded us to slay the giant. That is why we are here!"

Without waiting to hear any more, the princess ran up to Yorimitsu in her joy and clung to him, crying out in broken sentences: "Are you indeed the great Yorimitsu of whom I have so often heard? How thankful I am that you have come. I will be your guide to the giant's den. Hasten, warrior Yorimitsu, and kill the demons! I already feel that I am saved!"

When they heard these words the warriors knew that she was one of the giant's victims. The princess turned and led the way up the hill. Presently they saw a large iron gate guarded by two demons. The demon on the right was red and the demon on the left was black, and each was armed with a great iron stick or club. The princess whispered to Yorimitsu: "Behold the home of the giant. Enter the gates, and you will find a beautiful palace, built of black iron from the foundations to the roof. It is therefore called the Palace of Black Iron or Kurogane. It is large, and the inside is as beautiful as a great *daimyō*'s palace. Within the walls of the Palace of Black Iron, Shutendōji holds a feast night and day. He is waited upon by maidens such as I, whom he has carried off from the capital and from the provinces to be his slaves. The wine he drinks, poured out in crimson lacquer cups, is the blood of human beings, and the food of those feasts is the flesh of his victims who are slain in turn. What numbers have I seen disappear, alas! all murdered to supply the awful food and wine of those cannibal feasts. How I have prayed to Heaven to punish this monster! But when I saw the fate of my friends, how could I hope to live? I knew not when my turn would come. But since I have met you I feel that we shall all be saved and great is my joy and gratitude!"

By this time they had reached the gate, and the princess went forward and said to the red and black demon sentinels: "These poor travellers have lost their way on this mountain. I took compassion on them and brought them here, so that they may rest for a while before going on their journey. I hope you will be kind to them."

When the princess first began to speak the demons looked and saw Yorimitsu and his fellow priests. Little dreaming who these men were, and that in admitting them they were letting in the bravest warriors in the whole of Japan, and still less suspecting their purpose, the demons laughed in their hearts. Good prey had indeed fallen into their hands. They would surely be allowed a share in the feast that these fresh victims would furnish.

They grinned from ear to ear at the princess and told her that she had done well, and bade her take the six travellers into the palace and inform

Shutendōji of their arrival. Thus the six warriors entered into the very stronghold of the demons as if they were invited guests. Triumphant glee at the success of their plan made them exchange lightning glances with each other. They passed through the great iron gate, up to the porch, and then the princess led them through large spacious rooms and along great corridors till at last they reached the inner part of the palace. Here they were shown into a large hall. At the upper end in the seat of honor sat the demon king Shutendōji. Never had the warriors in their wildest dreams dreamt of such a hideous monster. He was ten feet in height, his skin was bright red and his wild shock of hair was like a broom. He wore a crimson *hakama*, and he rested his huge arms on a stand. As the warriors entered, he glared at them fiercely with eyes as big as a dish. The sight of this dread monster was enough to make any one tremble with fear, and had Yorimitsu and his warriors been weak they must have fainted away with horror.

Yorimitsu could hardly restrain himself from flying at the monster then and there, but he controlled himself and bowed humbly so as not to awaken the enemy's suspicion in any way.

Shutendōji, glaring at him, said haughtily: "I do not know who you are, or how you have found your way into this mountain, but make yourself at home!"

Yorimitsu and his men
come upon the giant

13

Then Yorimitsu answered meekly: "We are only humble mountain priests from Mount Haguro of Dewa. We were on our way to the capital, having been on a pilgrimage to the shrine of Omine. In travelling across these mountains we have lost our way. While wandering about and wondering which was the right path to take, we were met by one of the inmates of your palace and kindly brought here. Please pardon us for trespassing on your domains and for all the trouble we are giving you!"

"Don't mention it," said Shutendōji. "I am sorry to hear of your plight. Do not stand on ceremony while you are here, and let us feast together." Then turning to the attendant demons he shouted orders for the dinner to be served, and clapped his red hands together.

At this the partitions between the rooms slid apart and beautiful damsels magnificently robed came gliding in, bearing aloft in their hands large wine-cups, jars of *saké* and dishes of fish of all kinds, which they placed before the ugly giant and the guests. Yorimitsu knew that all these lovely princesses had been snatched from the Flower Capital by Shutendōji, who, heedless of their tears and misery, kept them here to be his handmaidens. He said to himself fiercely that they should soon be free.

Saké is passed around at the giant's court

Now that the wine-cups were brought in, the warrior seized his opportunity. From his satchel he took out the jar containing the enchanted wine he had received from the gods of the three shrines, and said to Shutendōji: "Here is some wine which we have brought from Mount Haguro. It is a poor wine and unworthy of your acceptance, but we have always found it of great benefit in refreshing us when we were weary from fatigue and in cheering our drooping spirits. It will give us much pleasure if you will try a little of our humble wine, though it may not please your taste!"

Shutendōji seemed pleased at this courtesy. He handed out a huge cup to be filled, saying: "Give me some of your wine. I should like to try it." The giant drained it at one swallow and smacked his lips over it.

"I have never tasted such excellent wine," he said and held out his cup to be filled again.

Yorimitsu was delighted, for he knew full well that the giant was given into his hand. But he dissembled cleverly and said as he filled the giant's wine-cup: "I am delighted that the Honorable Host should deign to like our poor country wine. While you drink, I and my companions will venture to amuse you by our dancing."

Then Yorimitsu made a sign to his men and they began to chant an accompaniment, while he himself danced.

Shutendōji was highly amused as well as his attendants. They had never seen men dance before, and they thought the strangers were very entertaining.

The goblins now began to pass the magic wine round and to grow merry. Others meanwhile whispered among themselves, pitying the six travellers who, all unconscious of the horrible fate which was about to overtake them, were spending their last hours of liberty and probably of life in giving wine to their slayers and in dancing and singing for their amusement!

Already the power of the enchanted wine had begun to work and Shutendōji grew drowsy. The wine in the jar never seemed to grow less, however much was taken from it, and by this time all the demons had helped themselves liberally. At last they all fell into a deep sleep, and stretching themselves out on the floor and on one another, some in one corner and some in another, they were soon snoring so loudly that the room shook, and were as insensible to all that was going on as logs of wood.

"The time has come!" said Yorimitsu, springing to his feet, and motioning to his men to get to work. One and all hastily opened their knapsacks. Taking out their helmets, their armour, and their long swords, they armed themselves. When they were all ready they all knelt down, and, placing their hands palm to palm, they prayed fervently to their patron gods to help them now in their hour of greatest need and peril.

As they prayed, a shining light filled the room, and in a radiant cloud the three deities appeared again. "Fear not, warrior Yorimitsu," they said. "We have tied the hands and feet of the giant fast, so you have nothing to fear. While your warriors cut off his limbs, do you cut off his head. Then kill the rest of the giant and your work will be done." The three old men then disappeared as mysteriously as they had come.

Yorimitsu rejoiced at the vision and worshipped with his heart full of gratitude the vanishing deities. The warriors then rose from their knees, took their swords and wet the rivets with water, so as to fix the blade firmly in the hilt. Then they all stole stealthily and cautiously towards Shutendōji. No longer the timid mountain priests, they were transformed into avenging warriors, clad in full armour. With flashing eyes and dauntless mien they moved across the room.

The captive princesses standing round realized that these men were deliverers, from their beloved capital. Their joy and wonder cannot be put into words. Some cried aloud with joy. Others covered their faces with their sleeves and burst into soft weeping. Others yet raised their hands to Heaven and exclaimed, "A Buddha come to Hell! Surely these brave men will kill the demons and set us free." And with clasped hands they entreated the warriors to slay their captors and take them back to their homes.

Now Yorimitsu stood over the sleeping Shutendōji with drawn sword, and raising it on high with a mighty sweep he aimed at the giant's neck, which was as big round as a barrel.

The head was severed from the body at one blow, but, horrible to relate, instead of falling to the ground, it flew up into the air in a great rage. It hung over Yorimitsu for a moment snorting flames of fire, and then swooped down as if it would bite off the warrior's head, but it was daunted by the glittering star on his helmet, and drew back and gazed in surprise at

the transformed man. Yorimitsu was scorched by the giant's flaming breath. Once more he raised his long sword and striking the terrible demon head brought it to the ground at last.

The noise of the combat and the triumphant shouts of the warriors awoke the other demons, who roused themselves as quickly as their stupefied senses allowed them. They were in a great fright, and without waiting to get their iron clubs, they made a rush upon Yorimitsu. But they were too late. His five braves dashed in and attacked them right and left, until in a few minutes there was not one left to tell the tale of the destruction which had come down upon them like the autumn whirlwind upon the leaves of the forest glades.

The captive princesses, when they saw that their captors were all slain, jumped about with gladness, waving their long sleeves to and fro, as the tears of joy streamed down their pale faces. They ran to Yorimitsu and caught hold of his sleeves and praised him, saying: "Oh! Yorimitsu Sama, what a brave and noble warrior you are! We are indeed grateful to you for having saved our lives. Never have we seen such a wonderful warrior." And with many such expressions of joy they gathered round the warrior, and their merry voices were now heard, instead of the groans of the dying cannibals.

The demon head snorts flames of fire

Yorimitsu enters the capital with his trophy

Now that Shutendōji was vanquished with all his horde, the way was quite open for Yorimitsu and his men to take the fair captives away from the castle of horror and make their way back to the capital as soon as possible.

First of all Yorimitsu tied up the head of Shutendōji with a strong rope and told the five brave warriors to carry it. Then, followed by the princesses, the little band left Mount Oe forever and set out on the homeward journey. When they reached Kyoto the news of Yorimitsu's return spread like fire, and the people came out in crowds to welcome the heroes.

When the parents of the long-lost damsels saw their daughters again, they felt as if they must be dreaming. It seemed too good to be true that the dear and cherished ones should be restored to them safe and well, and they overwhelmed Yorimitsu with praise and with precious gifts.

Yorimitsu took the head of Shutendōji to the emperor and told him of all that had happened to him. You may be sure that when His Majesty heard of the success which had crowned Yorimitsu and his expedition, he awarded him great praise and merit and bestowed upon him higher court rank than ever.

In all the country, far and near, Yorimitsu's name was in everyone's mouth, and he was acknowledged to be the greatest warrior in the land.

Even in the lonely country places there was not one poor farmer who did not know of the brave deeds of the great general.

Ever since then his portrait is familiar to the boys of Japan, for it is often painted on their kites.

Kidōmaru the Robber

You have just read of the brave warrior Yorimitsu's exploits at Oeyama and how he rid the country of the demons who haunted the city of Kyoto and terrified the inhabitants of the Flower Capital (as that city was sometimes called) by their terrible deeds.

It was not long after Yorimitsu's exploits at Oeyama that the country rang with the name of Kidōmaru, a robber and highwayman, who, by his notorious deeds of cruelty and robbery, had caused his name to be feared and hated by all, both young and old.

One evening Yorimitsu with his attendants was returning home from a day's hunting, when he happened to pass the house of his younger brother Yorinobu. The warrior had had a long day out. Having still a good distance to ride before he would reach his own house the thought of a good meal and friendly company, just then, when he was tired and very hungry, was pleasant to contemplate in the lonely hour of twilight. So he called a halt outside the house and sent in word to his brother that he, Yorimitsu, was passing by, and that if Yorinobu had any refreshment to offer his brother, he would call in and stay the night there, as he was tired out on his way back from a day's hunt.

Now in Japan an elder brother or sister commands respect from the younger members of the family, and so Yorinobu was very pleased that Yorimitsu, his elder brother, had called on him.

The servant soon returned with the message that Yorinobu was only too pleased to receive Yorimitsu. He had ordered a feast to be prepared that evening in honor of an unusual event, and as he was alone, nothing could be more opportune or give him greater joy than that his elder brother should have chanced to come by. He humbly begged Yorimitsu

Opposite page:
Kidōmaru the Robber

that he would deign to share the feast, such as it was, and to pardon the poorness of his hospitality.

Yorimitsu was very pleased with his brother's gracious reception. He quickly flung the reins to his groom, dismounted from his horse, and entered the house, wondering what could be the occasion of Yorinobu's ordering a banquet for himself. When the warrior was shown into the room he found Yorinobu seated on the mats drinking *saké*, as the servants were bringing in the first dishes of the dinner. When the salutations were over, Yorinobu handed Yorimitsu his wine-cup. Yorimitsu took it, and having drained it, asked what his brother meant by the feast he had promised him and what was the occasion of it. Yorinobu laughed as if with triumph, and wheeling round on his cushion pointed out into the garden.

Yorimitsu then looked in the direction indicated by his brother's hand, and saw, tied up to a large pine tree, a young man who could not be much over thirty and of extraordinary strength. The face of the captive expressed hate and ferocity, his body was of an enormous build, while his arms and legs were like trunks of pine trees, so large and brown and muscular were they. His hair was a rough and matted shock, and the eyes glared as if they would start from their sockets. Indeed to Yorimitsu the wild creature looked more like a demon than a human being.

"Well, Yorinobu!" said Yorimitsu, "the occasion of your feast is to say the least unusual. It must certainly have given you some sport to catch that wild creature. But tell me who he is that you have got tied up out there."

"Have you not heard of Kidōmaru, the notorious robber?" answered Yorinobu. "There he is! One of my men captured him out on the hills. He found him asleep. The town has long been clamoring for him. He has a big score to settle at last. For to-night I intend to keep him tied up like that, and to-morrow I shall hand him over to the law! Come, let us be merry, for the dinner is served!"

Yorimitsu clapped his hands when he heard of the great feat Yorinobu and his men had accomplished in catching the fearful robber, the terror of whose lawless deeds had long held the people of Kyoto trembling with fear and dread. The outlaw Kidōmaru was caught at last and by his own brother Yorinobu! This was an event of rejoicing and congratulation for the family.

"You have certainly done a meritorious service to your country," said he, "but it is ridiculous to tie such a creature up with a rope only. You might just as well think of tying up a wild cow with a fine kite-string. It would be less dangerous. Take my advice, Yorinobu, put a strong iron chain round him, or the murderer will soon be at large again."

Yorinobu thought his brother's advice wise, so he clapped his hands. When the servant came to answer the summons, he ordered him to bring an iron chain. When this was brought, he went into the garden, followed by Yorimitsu and his men, and wound it round Kidōmaru's body several times, securing it at last to a post with a padlock.

Kidōmaru up to this time had rejoiced at his light bonds. He was so strong that he knew he could easily break a rope, and he had waited but for the nightfall to make good his escape under cover of the darkness. You can imagine how great was his anger at Yorimitsu's interference, which was the cause of his being treated with so much severity that his projected escape would now be difficult.

"Hateful man!" muttered Kidōmaru to himself. "I will surely punish you for what you have done to me! Remember!" and he threw evil glances at Yorimitsu.

But the brave warrior cared little for the wild robber's malignant glances. He only laughed when he noticed them, and, as the chain was drawn tighter round the robber, he said: "That's right! That chain will hold him sure enough! You must run no risk of his escaping this time!"

Then he and Yorinobu returned to the house, and dinner was served and the two brothers made merry the whole evening, talking over old times, and it was late before they retired to rest.

Now Kidōmaru knew that Yorimitsu slept in Yorinobu's house, and he made up his mind to try to slay him that night, for he was mad with wrath at what Yorimitsu had done to him.

"He shall see what I can do!" growled Kidōmaru to himself, shaking his rough and shaggy head like a big long-haired terrier. He waited quietly till everyone in the house had gone to rest and all was silent. Then Kidōmaru arose, cramped and stiff from sitting tied up so long. With a mighty effort he flung out his great arms, laughing defiance at the chain that bound him.

So great was his strength that no second effort was needed. The chain broke and fell clanking to the ground at once, and Kidōmaru, like a large hound, shook himself free from his bonds. Softly as a mouse he approached the house and climbed on to the roof, and with one tremendous blow from his huge fist, he broke through the tiles and the boards to the ceiling. His plan was to jump down upon Yorimitsu while he lay sleeping, and taking him unawares suddenly to cut off his head. But the warrior had lain down to rest expecting such an attack, and he had slept but lightly. As soon as he heard the noise above him, he was wide awake in an instant, and to warn his enemy he coughed and cleared his throat. Kidōmaru was a man of fierce and dauntless character, and he was not in the least thrown back in his purpose by finding that Yorimitsu was awake. He went on with his work of making a hole large enough in the ceiling to let himself through to the room beneath.

Yorimitsu now sat up and clapped his hands loudly to summon his men, who slept in an adjoining room. Watanabe, the chief man-at-arms, came out to see what his master wanted.

"Watanabe," said Yorimitsu, "my sleep has been disturbed by something moving in the ceiling. It may be a weasel, for weasels are noisy creatures. It cannot be a rat, for a rat is not large enough to make so much noise. At any rate, it seems impossible to sleep to-night, so saddle the horses and get all the men ready to start. I will get up and ride out to the temple of Mount Kurama. I want all the men to accompany me."

Perched between the roof and the ceiling, the robber heard all this, and said to himself: "Yorimitsu goes to Kurama! That is good news! Instead of wasting my time here like a rat in a trap, I will set out for Kurama immediately and get there before those stupid men can, and I will waylay them and kill them all." So Kidōmaru crawled out on the roof again, let himself down to the ground, and hurried with all the speed he could make to Kurama.

A large plain had to be crossed in going from the city to Kurama, and here a number of wild cattle had their home. When Kidōmaru, on his way to Kurama, came to this spot, a plan flashed across his mind by which he could steal a march on Yorimitsu. He soon caught one of the big oxen a blow on the head. Three blows one after the other, and the ox fell dead at the robber's feet. Kidōmaru then proceeded to strip off its skin. It was very hard work, but he managed to do it quickly, so strong was he, and then throwing the hide over himself he lay down completely disguised, a man in a bull's hide, and waited for Yorimitsu and his men to come.

He had not long to wait. Yorimitsu, followed by his four braves, soon came in sight. The warrior reined in his horse when he came to the plain and saw the cattle. He turned to his men and said: "Here is a place where we may find some sport. Instead of going on to Kurama, let us stay here and have some hunting! Look at the wild cattle!"

The four retainers with one accord all gladly agreed to their chief's proposal, for they loved sport and adventure just as much as Yorimitsu and were glad of an excuse to show their skill as huntsmen. The sun was just rising, and the prospect of a fine morning added zest to the pastime. Each man prepared his bow and arrows in readiness to begin the chase.

But the cattle, thus disturbed, did not enjoy the sport. Man's play was their death indeed. One of their number had been killed by Kidōmaru, and now they were attacked by Yorimitsu and his men, who came riding furiously into their midst, shooting at them with bows and arrows. With angry snorts, whisking their tails on high and butting with their horns, they ran to right and left. In the general stampede that followed their attack, the hunters noticed that one animal lay still in the tall grass. At first they thought it must be either lame or ill, so they took no notice of it, and left it alone till Yorimitsu came riding up. He went up and looked at it carefully, and then ordered one of his men to shoot it.

The man obeyed, and taking his bow, shot an arrow at the recumbent animal. The arrow did not hit the mark. To the astonishment of the four hunters, the hide was flung aside and out stepped the robber Kidōmaru.

"You, Yorimitsu! It is you, is it?" he exclaimed. "Do you know that I have a spite against you?" And with these words he darted forward and attacked Yorimitsu with a dagger. But Yorimitsu did not even move in his saddle. He drew his sword and, adroitly guarding himself, exchanged two or three strokes with the robber, and then slashed off his head. But wonderful to relate, so strong was the will that animated Kidōmaru that though his head was cut off, his body stood up straight and firm till his right arm, still holding the dagger, struck at Yorimitsu's saddle. Then, and not till then, it collapsed.

It is said that the warriors were all greatly impressed by the malevolent spirit of the robber, which was strong enough to stir the body to action even after the head had been severed from the shoulders.

Such was the death of the notorious robber Kidōmaru, at the hands of the brave warrior Yorimitsu who was awarded much praise for the clever way in which he drew Kidōmaru out as far as Kurama to kill him. He had understood from Kidōmaru's evil glances that the robber planned to kill him, and he thus avoided causing trouble in his brother's house. In this instance, as always, Yorimitsu displayed wisdom and bravery.

No sooner was Kidōmaru killed, than news was brought to the capital that another man had arisen who imitated Kidōmaru in his daily deeds of robbery and other wicked acts. This robber's name was Kakamadare.

One bright moonlight night, Kakamadare was waiting on the plain between Kyoto and Kurama for travellers to come that way, hoping that luck would bring some rich man into his clutches. Presently he heard someone coming towards him playing on a flute. Thinking this somewhat strange, he hid himself in the grass and waited to see who would appear. The sweet music drew nearer and nearer, and then the player came in view. The light of the moon made everything as clear as day, and the robber saw a handsome samurai of warriorly aspect, dressed in beautiful silken robes and wearing a long sword at his side.

"Now's my opportunity; I'm in luck to-night," thought the robber, as he rose from his hiding-place and stealthily followed the flute-player. As he kept step by step behind him, Kakamadare drew his sword in readiness several times to cut down his prey, and waited for the chance to strike.

All at once the samurai turned and looked steadily at the robber, who began to tremble. Then the warrior calmly and coolly resumed his playing, as if utterly indifferent to the danger which threatened him. Once more the robber followed, with the intention of cutting the man down, but the opportunity for which he waited never came. Each time his hand went up with his sword, it as quickly fell to his side. A spirit of high and noble purpose seemed to emanate from the warrior, which cowed the man behind and made him weak. For so great is the virtue of the sword that in Japan it is an acknowledged fact that all noble swordsmen had this power of subduing

lesser natures by the spiritual grace which went forth from them. Indeed the belief in the occult power of the sword was great, and it was said that no bad man could keep the possession of a fine blade.

Kakamadare could not strike. He could not tell the cause of his weakness. He thought that it might be the influence of the music. He found himself listening to the gentle strains of the flute, and admiring the skill with which the man played. He noticed the firm and fearless air of the warrior as he walked and his great nerve. The man knew himself to be followed by a robber, yet he showed not the least concern. Kakamadare tried to turn back now, but he found that he could do nothing but follow the man in front of him. In this way the strange pair reached the town. Kakamadare now made a great effort to break the spell, and was on the point of turning back and

Kakamadare cannot strike

trying to escape from the strange, compelling presence, when to his astonishment the samurai suddenly wheeled round upon him and said: "Kakamadare, I thank you for your trouble! You have given me a safe escort!"

At this the robber became so terrified that he fell down on his knees and was unable to move or speak for some moments. At last, so soon as his tongue found utterance, he said: "I know not who you are, but I beg you to forgive me! I would have killed you!"

He then confessed everything to the warrior. He told him of his many deeds of robbery and violence which had made him feared and hated by the people, who thought that he must be a demon, for so cruel and relentless was he that he never showed mercy even to the poorest peasant. "I have never met any one like you," Kakamadare went on to say. "I promise to give up my life as a robber, and I beg you to take me into your service as one of the humblest of your retainers."

The warrior led the man home, and gave him some good clothes, telling him that when he again got into straits and wanted money or clothes, he might come a second time to the house, but that it was unwise to show such contempt for others as to enter into an encounter where he himself might be the injured party.

This kindness and mercy touched the man's heart, and from that day he became a reformed man and a law-abiding citizen.

The warrior was none other than Hirai Yasumasa, one of the warriors who accompanied Yorimitsu in his successful expedition against the giant of Oeyama. There is a saying that "Brave generals make brave warriors," and it is quite true. Yorimitsu was a man of great sagacity and courage, and his band of braves and the warrior Hirai, of whom we have just read, were like their master. There were no men in the whole of Japan braver than they. This proves the truth of the old adage.

The Monster Spider

There is another story about general Yorimitsu which you may like to hear. The sword with which Yorimitsu slew Kidōmaru was called the Kumokiri, or Spider-cutting Sword, and about the naming of this blade there is an interesting story.

It happened at one time that Yorimitsu was unwell and was obliged to keep to his room. Every night at about twelve o'clock a yong monk would come to his bedside, and in a kind and gentle way pour out and give him some medicine to take. Yorimitsu noticed that he did not know the boy, but as there were many underlings in the servants' quarters whom he never saw, this did not strike him as strange. But Yorimitsu, instead of recovering, found himself growing weaker and weaker, and especially after taking the medicine he always felt worse.

At last one day he spoke to his head servant and asked him who it was that brought him medicine every night, but the attendant answered that he knew nothing about the medicine and that there was no monk in the house.

Yorimitsu now suspected some supernatural snare. "Some malevolent being is taking advantage of my illness and trying to bewitch me or to cause my death. When the boy comes again to-night I will find out his real form. He may be a fox or goblin in disguise!" said Yorimitsu.

So he waited for the appearance of the monk, wondering what the strange incident could mean.

Yorimitsu (right) grows
weaker and weaker

源頼光土蜘蛛ヲ切ル圖

When midnight came, the boy, as usual, appeared, bringing with him the usual cup of medicine. The warrior calmly took the cup from the boy and said, "Thank you for your trouble!" but instead of swallowing the false medicine, he threw it, cup and all, at the boy's head. Then jumping up he seized the sword that lay beside his bed and cut at the impostor. As the blade fell, the monk screamed with rage and pain, then, with a movement as quick as lightning, before he turned to escape from the room, he threw something at the warrior, which, marvellous to relate, as he threw, spread outwards pyramidically into a large white sticky web which fell over Yorimitsu and clung to him so that he could hardly move. Yorimitsu whirled his sword round and cut the clinging meshes and freed himself. Again the monk threw a web over him, and again Yorimitsu cut the enmeshing threads away. Once more the huge spider's web—for such it was—was thrown over him, and then the spider fled. Yorimitsu called for his men and then sank exhausted on his bed.

His chief retainer, answering the summons, met the monk in the corridor, and thinking it strange that an unknown priest should come from his master's room at that hour of the night, stopped him with drawn sword.

The spider answered not a word, but threw his entangling web over the man and mysteriously disappeared.

Now thoroughly alarmed, the retainer hastened to Yorimitsu. Great was his consternation when he saw his master, with the meshes of the spider's web still clinging to him.

"See!" exclaimed Yorimitsu, pointing to the threads still clinging to his man and himself, "a monster spider has been here!"

He then gave orders to hunt down the spider, but the thing could nowhere be found. On the white mats and along the corridors they found as they searched red drops of blood, which showed that the creature had been wounded.

Yorimitsu's men followed the red trail, out into the garden, across the city to the hills, till they came to a cave, and here the blood-drops ceased. Groans and cries of pain issued from the cave, so the warriors felt sure that they had come to the end of their hunt.

"The spider is surely hiding in that cave!" they all said. Drawing their swords, they entered the cave and found a monster spider writhing with

Yorimitsu and his men come upon the spider

pain and bleeding from a deep sword-cut on the head. They at once killed the creature and carried it to Yorimitsu.

The warrior had often heard stories of these dreadful spiders, but had never seen one before.

"It was this monster spider then that wanted to prey upon me! The net that was thrown over me was a spider's web! Of all my adventures this is the strangest!" said Yorimitsu.

That night Yorimitsu ordered a banquet to be prepared for all his retainers in honor of the event, and he drank to the health of his five brave men.

From that time the monk never appeared and Yorimitsu recovered his health and strength at once.

Such is the story of the Kumokiri Sword. *Kumo* means "spider," and *kiri* means "cutting," and it was so named because it cut to death the monster spider who haunted the brave warrior Yorimitsu.

MINAMOTO YORIMASA

The Black Cloud

Long, long ago in Japan there lived a brave warrior named Minamoto Sanmi Yorimasa. Yorimasa was his own name, while Minamoto was the great clan to which he belonged, famous in history, and Sanmi showed that he was a warrior of the Third Rank at Court, from the word *san*, which means "three," and the word *i*, which means "rank."

Now Yorimasa is so celebrated a warrior that to this day his picture is painted on the kites which the little boys of Japan fly at the New Year, and if you visit the temple of the Goddess of Mercy, at Asakusa, in Tokyo, you will see his portrait even there. And at the Boys' Festival, on the fifth of the fifth month, when in every household where there are sons the favorite heroes of the land are set out in the alcove of honor of the guest-room, you will surely find amidst the martial show of toys the figure of an archer clothed from head to foot in gay armour, with a huge bow in his hand and a quiver full of arrows on his back. That is Yorimasa of brave and dear memory.

Yorimasa was the fifth descendant of the great warrior Yorimitsu, who killed the giant of Oeyama about whom you will soon read. As a youth Yorimasa was noted for his valor and his skill in archery, and he was soon called to the court and given the important post of Chief Guard of the Imperial Palace.

Though Yorimasa was a man of ability and the greatest archer of his time. And though he had done deeds of note which had brought him into

prominence, for some reason his rank at court remained stationary, and he did not advance from the Fourth Rank (*Shi-i*), which he had when he first entered the sacred precincts of the palace. The humor of the situation caught Yorimasa's fancy, for he was very quick-witted, and one day, smiling to himself, he sat down at his writing-table and composed a poem lamenting his bad luck. From the earliest ages the Japanese have trained themselves, at the times when their feelings are stirred by some event which causes happiness or sorrow or disappointment, not to give way to their emotions, but to control their minds sufficiently to compose a poem on the subject.

Yorimasa's poem was of thirty-one syllables, and in five short lines he said gracefully that "one who has not the means of climbing upwards remains under the tree and passes his life in picking up beechnuts." Now in Japanese the word for beechnuts is *shi-i*, and this word also means the Fourth Rank at Court. So that the couplet was a pun on his not being promoted. Yorimasa read the poem laughingly to some of his friends, and they, admiring his wit, repeated it and talked about it till it became quite famous in the palace, and at last reached the emperor's ear. The sympathy of His Majesty was aroused, and soon after this Yorimasa was raised to the Third Rank at Court, Sanmi, and by this title he has ever afterwards been known.

Now it happened that at this time the emperor became ill and could not sleep at night. He complained of disturbance and a great sense of oppression from sunset to sunrise. His courtiers, full of anxiety, sat up to watch the night through, to see if they could discover the cause of the emperor's agitation. Some kept vigil in and round the imperial chamber, others on the wide-eaved verandahs, and some in the courtyard of the palace. Then the watchers on the verandahs and in the courtyard noticed that as soon as the sun set a black cloud came from the eastern horizon of the capital, and travelling across the city finally rested on the roof of the palace called the Shin-shinden, or Purple Hall of the North Star, where the emperor slept. As soon as this cloud alighted on the palace, the emperor's sleep became disturbed, as if by frightful nightmare. Those in attendance round the royal bed heard strange scratchings and noises on the roof as if some dreadful beast were there. These unusual sounds and the nightmare of the imperial sleeper lasted till dawn, when it was noticed that the black cloud always withdrew.

智勇六佳選
源三位頼政

Now in the palace there was great commotion. The Minister of the Right and the Minister of the Left, whose duty it was to guard the emperor from all harm, held long and anxious consultation as to what should be done. Every one in the palace was of the opinion that the black cloud hid some monster which for some unknown cause haunted the emperor. It was quite certain that unless the monster were killed, and that soon, the emperor's life would be endangered, for he was growing weaker and thinner every day. The question was, who was brave enough to undertake the task? The palace sentinels were already scared, so it was useless to expect help from them. The ministers must seek for some brave samurai well known for his daring and his skill as an archer and put him on night-duty, charging him to kill the monster as soon as it should appear. The courtiers, one and all, said that Yorimasa was the man. An imperial messenger was therefore at once sent to the warrior, with a letter telling him what was demanded of him.

Yorimasa, when he read the letter, looked very grave, for he felt the responsibility of his new duty, which was different from all other work. On him now depended the recovery of the emperor, who was visibly growing worse and living through each day in terror of the nightmare which haunted him in the darkness.

Yorimasa was a man of great courage and resource, and lost not a moment in getting ready. He strung his best bow most carefully and placed his quiver in two steel-headed arrows. He then put on his armour, and over his armour he donned a hunting-dress, and to look more courtly he put on a ceremonial cap instead of a helmet. He chose his favorite retainer, the bravest and strongest of all his warriors, to accompany him. Yorimasa now set out as calmly and quietly as if he were simply going to his everyday duty and nothing more. As soon as his arrival was made known, he was summoned to the presence of the Ministers of the Right and the Left and told of all that was happening at court—how every night at the hour of sunset a black cloud was seen to issue from the east, approach the palace, and finally cover the roof of the Purple Hall of the North Star where the emperor always slept. Then the ministers told the warrior of the strange noises that were heard on the roof, of the howlings and scratchings which lasted all night till the dawn broke. It behooved him, they said, to do his best to kill the monster, if such it was, for all the guards were now thoroughly frightened, and none of them dared attack it in hand-to-hand fight, and none had skill enough to hit it in the dark, though the emperor's own body-guard of archers had tried again and again.

Yorimasa listened to the strange story gravely. He saw that the whole palace was in a state of alarm and disturbance, but he did not lose heart. With the greatest self-possession he waited for the end of the day. As soon as the sun set, the night grew stormy. The wind blew a hurricane, the lightning flashed, and the thunder roared. Nothing daunted by the fury of the elements, the brave archer waited and waited. It must have been near midnight when Yorimasa saw a thick black cloud sweep down and settle on the roof of the palace. He bade his retainer be ready with sword and torch at any moment and to follow him closely. The black cloud moved along the ridge of the grey-tiled roof till it stopped at the northeast corner, just over the imperial sleeping-chamber.

Yorimasa cautiously followed the movements of the cloud, his man just behind him. Straining his eyes, Yorimasa saw, during a vivid flash of lightning, the form of a large animal. Keeping his eyes on the spot where he had seen the head, while the peals of thunder crashed like cannon above, in the

Yorimasa confronts the
black cloud

Yorimasa shoots at the monster

darkness which followed he caught the glare first of one eye and then of the other as the creature moved along.

"This must be the monster who disturbs the emperor's rest!" said Yorimasa to himself.

With these words he fitted an arrow to the bow, and aiming to the left of where he saw the left eye glare he pulled his bow as round as the full moon and let fly. Yorimasa felt that his arrow had touched flesh. At the same moment there was a frightful howl and a heavy thud, and the writhing in agony of some animal on the ground, which showed that Yorimasa had done his work well.

Now Yorimasa's retainer rushed upon the monster. In one hand he held a blazing torch, in the other a short sword with which he stabbed the creature nine times and quickly despatched him. Then they both raised their voices and called to the sentinels and the courtiers to come and look. A strange sight was in store for them. Never had any of them seen anything like the monster that lay before them. The dreadful beast was as large as a horse. It had the head of an ape, the body and claws of a tiger, the tail of a serpent, the wings of a bird, and the scales of a dragon. They had heard and read of such creatures in some of the old books, but had always thought that such stories were old women's fables, to be told and whispered by grey-haired dames round the *hibachi* (fire-brazier) to their wonder-struck grandchildren, but never to be entertained seriously by men of sense. For a few moments they were all struck dumb with astonishment. They gazed silently first at the strange and horrible beast before them, then at Yorimasa, the slayer of it. Exclamations of wonder burst from their lips. Then one and all turned to the brave archer and congratulated him on his wonderful feat, his courage and his marksmanship. It seemed as if they would never cease applauding him.

The animal was flayed and its skin was carried to the emperor, who ordered it to be stored as a curiosity in the Imperial Treasure House. His Majesty was highly pleased. He sent for Yorimasa and bestowed on him a sword called Shishi-Ō, or the King of Lions. The time of the year was the beginning of the fifth month. The crescent moon hung like a silver bow in the twilight sky, and a *hototogisu* (cuckoo) was calling from the trees nearby. And thus the Minister of the Left who handed the sword to Yorimasa improvised the first half of a stanza saying:

O *hototogisu* of wonder,
even your name
Climbs ever upward
to the Heaven!

Then Yorimasa, with uplifted hands and bowed head, received the sword, and as he did so he completed the short poem with these words:

Not through thine own:
but through the merit
of a moon-shaped bow!

The Minister used the *hototogisu* then calling in the trees as simile of the brave warrior whose fame was rising now at court because of his brave deeds, and Yorimasa modestly answered that all was due not to his skill, but to his bow, which he likened to the crescent moon then reigning in the sky. Both

Yorimasa and Lady Ayame listen to the *hototogisu*

turned to the scenery of the moment for inspiration—the Minister in expressing his praise and the warrior in receiving it with humility and grace.

The emperor also considered this a fitting occasion to give Yorimasa the Lady Ayame (Iris) for his wife, and about this incident there is a pretty story.

Lady Ayame

The Lady Ayame was the most lovely lady-in-waiting in the palace, and as good as she was beautiful. Not only in beauty, but in mind and heart, was she superior to all the other ladies-in-waiting, and both the emperor and empress held her in high esteem. Many were the court nobles who fell in love with her, but all in vain. There was not one, however great or rich or handsome, who could make her so much as grant him even a fleeting smile. Time after time these noble suitors wrote her letters and poems, telling her of their hopeless love and beseeching her to send them but a single line in reply. But only her silence answered them. She remained obdurate to all entreaties.

One day Yorimasa, when on duty in the palace, caught a passing glimpse of the Lady Ayame, and from that hour his heart knew no rest. He could not forget the witching grace nor the modest beauty of her lovely face. Sleeping or waking the vision of his lady-love was always before his eyes, and it seemed to grow more vivid as the days went by. Time after time he wrote her letters and composed poems asking her to marry him, but the Lady Ayame treated Yorimasa as she treated all her other wooers—she vouchsafed him no reply. For three long years Yorimasa waited and hoped and despaired, and waited and hoped again, content if once in a way from a respectful distance he could catch a glimpse of her. In spite of long and cold discouragement he loved her perseveringly.

The emperor had heard of the warrior's constancy, and now sent for his favorite lady-in-waiting, thinking this the right time to reward Yorimasa's prowess and the Lady Ayame's merit, and to make them both happy.

As soon as Ayame appeared, His Majesty said: "Lady Ayame, is it true that you have received many letters from the warrior Yorimasa? Is it so?"

At this the Lady Ayame blushed like a peach-blossom in the glow of dawn, and hesitating a moment she replied: "May it please the Son of Heaven to condescend to send for Yorimasa and ask him!"

His Majesty then commanded her to retire, and forthwith summoned Yorimasa into his presence.

It was the fifth of May, the Spring Festival, and Yorimasa came robed in gala attire. He presented himself below the dais on which the emperor was seated and prostrated himself before the throne.

"Is it true," and the emperor smiled as he spoke, "that you love the Lady Ayame?"

Yorimasa was bewildered by the suddenness of the question and knew not what to reply, for he knew it to be strictly forbidden by court etiquette to write love-letters to any lady-in-waiting, and he had done this persistently.

Now the emperor saw Yorimasa's confusion and felt sorry for him. A bright thought struck His Majesty. He would please and puzzle Yorimasa and have some fun at his expense at the same time as well. He whispered an order to the chief master of ceremony.

In a short time three ladies appeared, heralded by attendants. As they moved across the mats of the immense hall, Yorimasa saw that they were all dressed exactly alike, and that even their hair was done in the same style, so that it would be impossible for any one who did not know them well to distinguish one from the other.

Who were they? Was the Lady Ayame one of them?

Like maidens of heaven (*tennin*) did the three noble damsels appear and their robes were beautiful to behold. So alike were they, and their beauty so extraordinary, that Yorimasa compared them to plum-blossoms on a branch seen through a window.

"The Lady Ayame is here," said the emperor. "Choose her from among three ladies and take her."

Yorimasa bowed to the ground. He was overcome with the graciousness and kindness of the emperor. But the task laid upon him he felt to be too difficult. Being a military man and inferior in rank to the court circle, Yorimasa had never had an opportunity of seeing any of the court ladies face to face. All he had seen of the Lady Ayame was sometimes a glimpse of her from the courtyard, where he was stationed, as she passed along the corridors of the palace. Once at a poetical party, to which he had been admitted as a great favor, he had seen her, at the further end of the hall, glide with trailing robes of ceremony into her place behind the silken screen which always hid the women from view at such gatherings. That was all he had ever seen of her, so that now he could not distinguish her from the rest.

The emperor was pleased at the success of his pleasantry. He saw that Yorimasa was fairly perplexed, and that he was unable to pick out his lady-love from her companions.

"I am a warrior and no courtier," thought the warrior, "I may not presume to lift my eyes to a lady of the court. Nor can I be sure which is Ayame. Were I to make a mistake and choose the wrong lady, it would be a lifelong disgrace and disappointment to me!"

The perplexity in his mind at once rose to his lips in the form of a short poem, which he repeated:

> In the rainy season,
> when the waters overflow
> the banks of the lake,
> who can gather the Iris?"

雪月花
都　京　御所月
源三位頼政　菖蒲の前　左大臣頼長

By the rainy season Yorimasa meant his three years of hopeless courting, during which his eyes had become dim with the tears of disappointment he had shed, so that he could no longer see clearly enough to discover which was the lady of his choice. In this way he excused himself for his seeming stupidity, and showed a modest reserve which pleased all present.

The aptness and quickness of Yorimasa's verse won the emperor's admiration. The tears stood in the august eyes, for he thought of the great love wherewith Yorimasa had loved the Lady Iris, and of the sorrow and patience of his long wooing and waiting. His Majesty rose from his throne, descended the steps of the dais, and going up to Ayame took her by the hand and led her forth to Yorimasa.

"This is the Lady Ayame, I give her to you!" were the golden words of the emperor.

To Yorimasa it must have seemed too wonderful almost to be true. The great desire of his life was given him by the emperor himself!

Then Yorimasa led his beautiful lady-love away and married her, and we are told that they lived as happily as fish in water. And it seemed as if they had but one heart between them, so harmonious was their union. In the palace there was great rejoicing over the auspicious event, and all the courtiers praised the merit of the verse which had finally given Ayame to Yorimasa and won the emperor's special commendation. The happy couple received the congratulations of the emperor and empress, of the courtiers and many noble people, and wedding-presents innumerable. Surely at this time there was no one happier than Yorimasa in all the land.

The Mikoshi

There are many stories told of Yorimasa which show us that he was not only a brave warrior and a man of learning and a poet, but also a man of wit and tact who knew how to use men as he willed.

Now one day a band of discontented turbulent priests came to the palace gate where Yorimasa was on guard, and demanded entrance. It must be explained that in those days the Buddhist priests of Kyoto were a set of wild and lawless men who often brought shame to their religion by their wicked lives. They lived outside the city on Mount Hiei, which they made their stronghold, and, forgetting the dignity of their religion, they took sides in war and in politics. They gave trouble to those in authority, especially to those who did not favor them. They used the smallest event as an occasion for carrying swords and bows and arrows, and it was their habit to go out equipped like warriors going forth to war.

Yorimasa saw that the priests were all well armed, and only too anxious to find a pretext for drawing their swords. They carried with them in great state the *mikoshi* (sacred palanquin) of their temple. In this *mikoshi* their patron god was supposed to dwell, and it was borne aloft on the shoulders of fifty men. With loud shoutings and a wild display of strength the priests

A *mikoshi* is carried through the streets of the capital

rushed the car along, now lifting it high above their heads, now staggering under its weight, as it seemed about to crush them to the ground.

Now Yorimasa was in no mood for fighting that day, and it seemed to him not worth his while to set his men—the best fighters and archers in the realm—against a handful of priests whom he could disperse in a few minutes. Besides, these priests from Mount Hiei were troublesome fellows and he did not wish to earn their enmity. So laughing quietly to himself he said that he would have some fun at their expense.

When the procession stopped opposite the gate, Yorimasa with his captains of the guard sallied forth to meet the noisy crowd, and coming in front of the *mikoshi* bowed in reverence before it with slow ceremony.

The priests, who had expected and were prepared for a very difficult reception, were surprised and somewhat taken aback. After some parley amongst themselves, their spokesman advanced and asked leave to enter the gate, saying they had a petition to present to the emperor.

Yorimasa sent his captain forward.

"My lord bids you welcome," he said, "and wishes me to say that he worships the same god as yourselves, and he is therefore averse to shooting against the *mikoshi* with his bows and arrows. Besides this, we are very few in number, so that your names will be dishonored and you will be called cowards for having chosen the weakest post to fight. Now the next gate is guarded by the Taira warriors, who are much stronger in numbers than we are. How would it do for you to go round and fight there? You would surely gain glory in an encounter with them."

The priests were so pleased by the flattery of this speech that they did not see that it was a ruse on the part of Yorimasa to get rid of them easily, and that he was sending them round to bother his rivals. He had also appealed to their best feelings, for Japanese chivalry teaches that in the event of choosing between two enemies the weaker must always be spared.

Some polite answer was made to Yorimasa, and then the priests shouldered the *mikoshi* and departed in the same spirited and vociferous manner that they had come. They went to the next gate, guarded by the Taira. Battle was given at once, for they were refused admittance. The priests were beaten and fled for their lives to the hills.

Uji Bridge

All these stories show us that Yorimasa was a clever man in every way, but in the end he was unfortunate, and for this there was no help.

When we read the story of his ill-fated death our hearts are filled with sorrow for him. It is not always as one wishes in this world, and Yorimasa did not meet with the fate his meritorious deeds and character deserved.

The Taira clan were now in the ascendant (Yorimasa, it will be remembered, belonged to the Minamoto), and Kiyomori, their despotic and unprincipled leader, was Prime Minister. All the important posts in the Bakufu he gave to his sons, grandsons, and relations, who under these circumstances, seeing that they owed everything to him, did just as the tyrant ordered. All samurai who did not belong to the Taira clan he treated unjustly, even throwing those he did not like into prison, whether they were innocent or guilty of the crimes or behavior deserving such punishment.

As a general of the rival Minamoto clan, Yorimasa suffered much from this unfair treatment. As he watched the arrogant conduct of Kiyomori and his son Munemori, he longed to be able to punish them and to bring retribution on the whole clan, and to this end he thought and worked and planned.

At last the Taira became so overbearing and so powerful that their actions passed the bounds of all reason, and Kiyomori, on a question of succession to the throne, confined the reigning emperor in his palace.

This last step was too much for Yorimasa. He could endure this state of things no longer, and he resolved to make a bold strike for the right. He placed Prince Takakura, the son of the late emperor, at the head of his army and set out to do battle with the Taira.

But the Minamoto were far inferior in numbers to the Taira, and, sad to relate, Yorimasa was defeated in his good and just cause. With the remainder of his army he fled before the enemy and took refuge in the Byōdō-in, the ancient monastery situated on the Uji River.

The Byōdō monastery, a large edifice near Kyoto, remains to this day. Here Yorimasa made a last stand to afford time for Prince Takakura to escape. He divided his men into two parties—one division he stationed as a reserve

Yorimasa (right) conducts his men into battle at the Uji bridge

force in the grounds of the monastery, while the other he drew up in battle array along the banks of the river. In case of pursuit, to prevent the enemy from crossing the river, they tore up the planks which formed the flooring of the bridge, so that only a skeleton of posts and cross-beams remained. Then they rested and waited to see what would happen.

The Taira soon came in sight following hard after them. First came the generals, then the warriors, twenty-eight thousand strong. They approached the bridge, but stopped short when they saw what the Minamoto had cleverly done. In a few minutes they ranged themselves along the bank facing the enemy.

Both armies now stood confronting each other on either side of the Uji River. Simultaneously the order was given to fight by both the Minamoto and the Taira generals and a fierce discharge of arrows from both sides ensued.

Then there rushed forth from the ranks of the Minamoto a huge priest, Tajimabō by name (in those days the Buddhist priests often took part in battles). Brandishing an enormous halberd he dashed out alone on the skeleton bridge. The Taira, thinking that he made an excellent target, shot a shower of arrows at him, but he was not in the least daunted. When the arrows were aimed at his head, he stooped and they passed over him. When they were aimed at his legs, he jumped high in the air and they flew under him. When they were aimed at his body, he swept them aside with his halberd. In this way he escaped free from hurt. So quick was he in his movements, and so marvellous was the way in which he balanced himself in his progress across the bridge, that he seemed to be endowed with power more than human. And not only his own comrades but the enemy also looked at him in breathless admiration.

Then another of Yorimasa's men, also a priest, Jōmyō by name, inspired by this example, came forth and stood up at the end of the bridge, and fitting his arrows to the bow, in rapid succession shot about a dozen of the foe, in the twinkling of an eye.

Crying out, "Oh, this is too much trouble!" he threw away his bow and arrow, and walked over the bridge on another beam, sweeping aside with his sword the arrows aimed at him.

Yet another priest, famous for his great strength, dashed out and followed after his friends across the bridge. He soon came up with Jōmyō, but as the beams of the bridge were narrow he could not pass him. Stopping for a moment to think what he should do, he stretched out his hands and touched

Warriors do battle on the beams of Uji bridge

the helmet of the man just in front of him, then lightly and quickly jumped leap-frog over his head. The bridge was now soon swarming with the Minamoto, who with fierce battle-cries began to attack the Taira, whose advance was entirely checked. For some minutes the Taira were greatly put out, not knowing what to do.

Then one brave youth, seeing how matters stood, and that it required someone to take a dauntless lead, sprang forth in front of the Taira and called out: "Now that it comes to this, there is no other way!" and with these words he dashed his horse into the river. It was the rainy season, and the waters were higher and the current stronger than usual. Black with mud the river ran swirling and whirling on its course.

Never was there a braver sight than when the young warrior drove his horse into the swollen river and made for the other side. His comrades could not stand still and watch him. Fired by his courage, numbers of the Taira, shouting "I also! I also!" dashed in after him. In a few minutes, while the Minamoto looked on in surprise, three hundred men had followed the gallant young captain, stemmed and crossed the torrent, and landed on the other side. And with the same dashing spirit, carrying everything before them, they broke through the last lines of the Minamoto and entered the Byōdō monastery, where their last stand was made. The Minamoto, with Yorimasa at their head, were now in a desperate condition. Seeing his father hard-pressed, Kanetsuna, Yorimasa's second son, an intrepid young warrior, rushed into the thickest of the fight and tried to defend his father. A Taira captain coming up with fifteen of his men seized Kanetsuna, overpowered him, and cut off his head.

Not one of Yorimasa's little band turned to flee. Although they knew there was no hope, they fought on face to face with the foe, for samurai traditions held it a disgrace to be even wounded in the back. One famous general in ancient history issued an order to the effect that prizes would be awarded to those who were shot in the forehead, but those who were wounded in the back should be slain.

One by one, the Minamoto fell, slain either by sword or arrow. Yorimasa received several wounds. Then he saw that there was no use in fighting any more; all was lost. Those of the Minamoto who were still left made a brave

stand round their chieftain. While they kept the enemy at bay Yorimasa slipped away and hastened to Prince Takakura, in the monastery, and begged him to flee in safety while there was yet time.

Having seen his imperial master safe, Yorimasa then retired to an inner part of the garden, and sitting under a large tree drew out his sword and prepared himself to commit *harakiri*, for samurai honor would not let him survive defeat. Calling his retainer Watanabe, who had escaped unhurt and who never left his master's side, Yorimasa bade him act as second in the rite. Then quietly taking off his armour, he composed a poem. He likened himself to a fossil tree that never knows the joy of blossoming, for he had never attained his ambition (the destruction of his enemies), "and sad indeed is the end of my life," the last line of the verse, were the last words he uttered.

He took out his short sword, and thrusting it into his side died like a brave and gallant samurai, without a moan. Then from behind, as was his duty as second, Watanabe cut off his master's head, and so that it should not be discovered by the enemy and carried away as a trophy of war, he tied a large stone to it, and with sorrowful reverence dropped it into the river and watched it sink beneath the water out of sight.

In this way Yorimasa died. Those of his followers who were not killed by the enemy died by their own hand, and Prince Takakura, fleeing to Nara, was overtaken by the Taira and put to death on the way.

Yorimasa was seventy-five years of age when he died. Though, as he lamented in his last poem, he had not achieved his ambition in punishing the Taira, yet years later his work was carried on, and the Taira were wiped out by Yoritomo, the great chieftain and mighty avenger of the Minamoto. And the name of Minamoto Sanmi Yorimasa lives forever in the history of his country.

MINAMOTO TAMETOMO

A Wild Youth

Long, long ago there lived in Japan a man named Hachirō Tametomo, who became famous as the most skilful archer in the whole of the realm at that time. Hachirō means "the eighth," and he was so called because he was the eighth son of his father, general Tameyoshi of the house of Minamoto. Yoshitomo, who afterwards became such a great figure in Japanese history, was his elder brother. Tametomo was therefore uncle to the *Shōgun* Yoritomo and the hero Yoshitsune, of whom you will soon read. He belonged to an illustrious family indeed.

As a child Tametomo gave promise of being a very strong man, and as he grew older this promise was more than fulfilled. He early showed a love of archery, and his left arm being four inches longer than his right, there was no one who could bend a bow better or send an arrow farther than he could. By nature Tametomo was a rough, wild boy who did not know fear, and he loved to challenge his elder brothers to fight. He grew ever wilder as he grew older, till at last he acted so rudely and wilfully, respecting and obeying no one set over him, that even his father found him unmanageable.

Now it happened when Tametomo was thirteen years old that a learned man, named Fujiwara no Shinsei, came to the palace of the emperor one day to give a lecture on a certain book. During the lecture he said that there could not be found in the whole of Japan a warrior whose skill in archery could match that of Kiyomori, the chieftain of the Taira clan, or of Yorimasa,

the Minamoto warrior. These two warriors, though belonging to two differ-ent clans, were the best archers throughout the land. Now Tametomo, when he heard these words, laughed aloud in scorn, and said, so that everyone might hear him, that Fujiwara no Shinsei was right about Yorimasa, but to call their enemy, that coward of a Kiyomori, a clever archer, only showed what a foolish and ignorant man Fujiwara no Shinsei was.

This rude speech, so contrary to the rules of Japanese courtesy, which com-mands young people to maintain a respectful and humble silence in the pres-ence of their elders, made Shinsei very angry. When the lecture was finished, he therefore sent for Tametomo and rebuked him sternly for his behavior, but the daring Tametomo, instead of being ashamed of his unmannerly conduct and prostrating himself in apology before the learned man, would not listen to anything he had to say, and was so boisterous in declaring that he was right that Fujiwara gave up his task of correction as a hopeless one.

But the lad's father, Tameyoshi, when he heard of what had happened, was very angry with his son for daring to dispute with his elder and superior, especially in the sacred precincts of the palace. He was so angry indeed that at last he refused to see him or to keep him any longer under his roof, and to punish him he sent him far away from his home to the island of Kyushu.

Now Tametomo, like the wilful, headstrong boy that he was, did not mind his banishment at all. On the contrary, he felt like a hound let loose from the leash, and rejoiced in his liberty, even though he had incurred his father's displeasure.

When he reached the island of Kyushu he made his way to the province of Higo, and finally settled down in the plain of Kumamoto. Tametomo found himself free to do just as he liked, his thirst for conflict became so great that he could not restrain himself. He gathered round him a band of fighters as wild as himself and challenged the men in all the neighboring provinces to come out and match their strength against his. In the twenty battles that followed Tametomo was never once defeated, so great was his strength, and his cleverness in directing his warriors. He was like a silkworm eating up the mulberry tree. Just as the silkworm devours one leaf after another, with slow but sure relentlessness, so Tametomo fought the inhabitants of the provinces round about till he had brought them all into subjection under him. By the

time he was eighteen years old he had made himself chief of a large band of outlaws, distinguished for their reckless bravery, and with them he had mastered the whole of Kyushu, the western part of Japan. It was now that the name of Chinsei was given him on account of his having conquered the west (*chin* meaning "to put down," and *sei* "west") .

Tidings travelled slowly in those days, and all carrying of news was done on foot by messengers. So a long time passed before the Bakufu at the capital heard of the wild and lawless doings of Chinsei Hachirō Tametomo, but at last his daring exploits became known, and the Bakufu decided to interfere and to put a stop to his outlawry. They sent a regiment of warriors to hunt him down and take him prisoner, but Tametomo and his band were not only strong and fearless, but sharp of wit, and in the frequent skirmishes that took place they always came out victorious. At last the warriors gave up their task of capturing him, for they found it impossible to overcome him and nothing would make Tametomo surrender. So the general returned to the capital and confessed that his expedition had failed. The Bakufu now decided to arrest the outlaw's father, Tameyoshi, and so try to bring the rebel to bay. Tameyoshi was therefore seized and punished for being the parent of such an incorrigible rebel.

Now even the wilful Tametomo was moved and distressed when he heard of what had happened to his father, because of him. Though undisciplined by nature, and ever ready to rebel against all authority, yet hidden deep in his heart was still a sense of duty to his father, and on this his enemies had counted. He knew that it was inexcusable to let his father suffer punishment for his misdoings. As soon as the bad tidings reached him, he gave up without the least hesitation all the land in Kyushu, which had cost him several years of hard fighting to wrest from the inhabitants, and taking with him only ten of his men, with all the speed he could make, he went up to the capital.

As soon as he reached the city he sent in a document signed and sealed in his blood, asking pardon of the Bakufu for all his former offenses, and begging that his father might be released at once. He then waited calmly and quietly for his sentence of punishment to be declared.

Now when those in authority saw his filial piety and his good conduct at this crisis, they could not find it in their hearts to treat him with severity.

"Even this man who has behaved like a demon can feel so much for his father," they exclaimed. And merely rebuking him for his lawlessness they handed him over to his father, whom they had set free.

At this time civil war broke out in the land, for two brothers, sons of the late ex-Emperor Toba, aspired to sit on the imperial throne. Owing to the favoritism of their father the elder brother, Sutoku, was forced to abdicate and retire, while Go-Shirakawa, the younger brother, was put on the throne. On his deathbed the ex-Emperor Toba (also called the Pontiff-Emperor) had foreseen that there would be strife between the two, and left sealed instructions in case of emergency. On opening this document it was found to contain a command to all the principal generals to support Go-Shirakawa.

Hence the great chieftain of the Taira, Kiyomori, and Tametomo's eldest brother, Yoshitomo—indeed all the warriors of repute and strength—supported Go-Shirakawa, while such nobles as Yorinaga and Fujiwara no Shinsei, who knew nothing of fighting, sided with the retired Emperor Sutoku. Yorinaga, it is said, could not mount his horse. Indeed the only efficient warriors on Sutoku's side were Tameyoshi and his seven younger sons, Tametomo, the reformed rebel, amongst them. Sutoku was told of Tametomo's strength

Kiyomori, the great chieftain of the Taira clan

and wonderful skill as an archer, and was advised to make use of him, so Tametomo was summoned to the ex-emperor's presence.

Tametomo was now just twenty years of age. He was more than seven feet in height, his eyes were sharp and piercing like those of a hawk, and he carried himself with great pride and noble bearing. As he entered the Imperial Audience Hall, so strong and brave and such a fine warrior did he look, that Sutoku at once felt confidence in him, and without delay consulted the young warrior about the impending war.

Then Tametomo told the emperor of how, when he had been banished to the west by his father, he had lived the life of an outlaw for many years—all that time his hand had been raised against everyone, and everyone had fought against him. It had been his delight and pastime to fight all who opposed his being lord of Kyushu. He and his band had always conquered, he said, because they had always fought at night. It would be a good plan, he thought, for Sutoku and his men to attack the Shirakawa palace by night, to set fire to the palace on three sides and to place warriors on the fourth side to seize the new emperor and his party when they tried to escape. If the ex-emperor would follow his advice, Tametomo said he felt sure that he would win the victory.

Yorinaga, who was attending the council when he heard Tametomo's plan, shook his head in disapproval, and said that Tametomo's scheme of attack was an inferior one. In his opinion it was a coward's trick to attack by night, and it was more befitting brave warriors to fight by day in the traditional way. When Tametomo saw that his advice was overruled and that Sutoku's council would not follow his tactics, he left the palace.

When he reached home he told his men of all that had passed, and added in his anger that Yorinaga was a conceited fellow who knew nothing of fighting, though he had dared to give his worthless opinion and to contradict him, Tametomo, who had fought without once being beaten all his life long. Thus giving vent to his disappointment, Tametomo seated himself on the mats, and as his anger passed away, he added with a sigh: "I only fear that Sutoku will be defeated in the coming struggle!"

Had Tametomo's tactics been followed, Japanese history would certainly have been different, for Kiyomori and Yoshitomo won a victory by the very plan which Tametomo had advised Sutoku to follow.

That night, without any warning, the enemy attacked the Shirakawa Palace.

The wary Tametomo expected an assault and had stationed himself at the south gate on guard. On seeing Kiyomori and his band approaching he exclaimed: "You feeble worms! I'll surprise you!" and taking his bow and arrow shot a samurai named Itō Roku through the breast. The arrow was shot with such skill and force that it went right through the warrior's body, and coming out through his back, pierced the sleeve of the armour of Itō Go, his younger brother, who was riding close behind him.

Itō Go, when he saw the precision and strength with which the arrow was shot, knew that this was no common foe, and in alarm carried the arrow to his general, Kiyomori, to show it to him. Kiyomori examined the arrow carefully and found that it was made from a strong bamboo of more than the usual thickness, and that the metal head was like a big chisel, a formidable weapon indeed! It was so large that it resembled a spear more than an arrow, and even the redoubtable Kiyomori trembled at the sight of it.

"This looks more like the arrow of a demon than of a man. Let us find another place of assault where our enemies are weaker and where the leaders are not such remarkable marksmen!" said he.

Kiyomori then retired from the attack on the south gate.

When Yoshitomo (who was now supporting Kiyomori, though later on he left the Taira chieftain) heard of his brother Tametomo's doings, he said: "Tametomo may be a daredevil and boast of his skill as an archer, but he will surely not take up his bow and arrow against the person of his elder brother," and he took Kiyomori's place at the south gate of the palace which Tametomo was guarding.

Drawing near the great roofed gate, Yoshitomo called aloud to Tametomo and said: "Is that you, Tametomo, on guard there? What a wicked deed you commit to fight against your elder brother? Now quickly open the gate and let me in. Tametomo! Do you hear? I am Yoshitomo! Retire there!"

Tametomo laughed aloud at his elder brother's command and answered boldly: "If it is wrong for me to take up arms against you, my brother, are you not an undutiful son to take up arms against your father?" (Tameyoshi, his father, was fighting on the ex-emperor's side.)

Yoshitomo had no words wherewith to answer his brother and was silent. Tametomo, with his archer's eye, saw what a good mark his brother made just outside the gate, and he was greatly tempted to shoot at him even for sport. But he said that though war found them fighting on opposite sides, yet they were brothers, born of the same mother, and that it would be acting against his conscience to kill or hurt his own brother, for surely he would do so if he took aim seriously! He would however for the sake and love of showing Yoshitomo what a clever marksman he was. Taking good aim at Yoshitomo's helmet, Tametomo raised his bow and shot an arrow right into the middle of the star that topped it. The arrow pierced the star, came out the other side, and then cut through a wooden gate five or six inches in thickness.

Even Yoshitomo was astonished at the skill which his brother displayed by this feat of archery. He now led his warriors forward to the attack.

But Sutoku's army was far outnumbered by the enemy, who swept down upon the palace in overwhelming numbers, and though Tametomo fought bravely and with great skill, his strength and valor were of no avail against the great odds which assailed him. The enemy gained ground slowly, inch by inch, till at last the gates were battered down, and they ruthlessly entered

Tametomo takes aim at
Yoshitomo's helmet

the palace. Calamity was added to calamity, the foe set fire to several parts of the building, and great confusion ensued.

The ex-emperor, in making a vain attempt to escape with Yorinaga, was caught and taken prisoner. Seeing that for the present there was nothing to be done, Tametomo, with his father Tameyoshi and his other brothers, all loyal to Sutoku's cause, made good their escape and fled to the province of Omi.

Tameyoshi was an old man unable to endure the hardships of a hunted life, and he found that he could go no further. So he told his sons that, as the emperor had been taken prisoner, and as there was no hope of raising Sutoku's flag again, at any rate for the present, it would be wiser for them all to return to the capital and surrender themselves to the conquerors—the Taira. They all agreed to this proposal except Tametomo, so Tameyoshi, the aged general, and the rest of his sons went back to Kyoto.

Now Tametomo was left behind, alone in his brave resolution to fight another battle for the ex-Emperor Sutoku. As soon as he had parted, sad and determined, from his father and brothers, he made his way towards the eastern provinces. But unfortunately, as he was journeying, the wound he had received in the recent fight became so painful that he stopped at some springs along the route, with the hope that the healing waters, a panacea for so many ills in Japan, would heal his hurt. But while taking the cure, his enemies came upon him and made him prisoner and he was sent back a captive to the capital. By the time Tametomo reached the city, his father and his brothers had been put to death, and he was soon told that he was to meet the same cruel fate.

But courage always arouses chivalry in the hearts of friends and foes alike, and it seemed to Tametomo's enemies a pity to put such a brave man to death. In the whole land there was no man who could match him in bending the bow and sending the arrow home to its mark, so it was decided to spare his life at the last moment. But to prevent him from using his wonderful skill against them, his enemies cut the sinews of both his arms and sent him away to the island of Oshima off the coast of the province of Izu live. Lest he should escape on the way they bound him hand and foot and put him in a palanquin. He was surrounded by a guard of fifty men, and so big and heavy was he that twenty bearers were required to carry the palanquin.

In spite of all the misfortunes that had befallen him, he carried the same courage, the same stout merry heart, the same love of wildness with him, even into exile. As the twenty men carried him along in the palanquin, Tametomo just for fun would now and again put forth all his strength. So great was his weight then that the twenty bearers would stagger and fall to the ground. These feats of strength alarmed the escort of fifty warriors. They feared lest he should act more savagely and become unmanageable, past their power of control, so they treated him in much the same way as they would have treated a lion or a tiger. They tried not to anger him, but did their utmost to keep him in a good humor during the journey.

At last they reached the province of Izu and the seashore from where they had to cross over to the island. Here they hired a boat, and putting Tametomo safely on board they took him to his last destination and left him there.

Though Tametomo was banished to this island, once there his enemies left him free to do as he liked. He was not treated as a common prisoner, but as a brave though vanquished foe. The simple islanders recognized in

him a great man and behaved to him accordingly and listened to everything
he chose to say. So he led an unmolested life, free from care, except the sorrow of being an exile—but his was a nature which took life as it came, without worrying about what he could not help.

Strange Creatures

One day Tametomo was standing on the beach gazing out to sea, thinking of
the many adventures he had passed through and wondering if fate would
ever bring any change in the quiet life he was leading, when he saw a sea-
gull come flying over the water. At first Tametomo with his keen eyes saw
only a speck in the distance, but the speck grew larger and larger till at last
the seabird appeared. Tametomo guessed that there was an island lying in
the direction from which the bird came. So he got into a boat and set out on
a voyage of discovery.

As he expected, he came to an island, after sailing from sunrise to sun-
down. To his amazement he found the place inhabited by creatures very different from human beings. They had dark red faces, with shocks of bright
red hair, the locks of which hung over their foreheads and eyes. They looked
just like demons. A whole crowd of these alarming-looking creatures were
standing on the beach when Tametomo landed. When they caught sight of
him they talked and gesticulated wildly amongst themselves and with fierce
looks they rushed towards him.

Tametomo saw at once that they meant him harm, but he was not at all
daunted. He went up to a large pine tree that was growing nearby, laid his
hands on it, and uprooting it with as much ease as if it were a weed, he brandished it over his head and called aloud threateningly: "Come, you demons,
fight if you will. I am Chinsei Hachirō Tametomo, the Archer of great Japan.
If you will henceforth become my servants and look up to me as master in
all things, it is well; otherwise I will beat you all to little pieces."

When the demons saw Tametomo's great strength and his fearlessness
they trembled. They held a short parley amongst themselves, and then the
demon chief stepped forward, followed by all his band. They came in front

of Tametomo and prostrating themselves before him on the sand, they one and all surrendered. Tametomo with much pride took possession of this island of demons and made himself monarch of all he surveyed. Having subdued the demons he returned to Oshima with the news. Great was the praise and merit awarded him by all the islanders.

Another day, soon after this, Tametomo was walking along the sands of the seashore, when he saw coming towards him, floating nearer and nearer on the top of the waves, a little old man. Tametomo could hardly believe what he was seeing; he had never seen anything so strange in his whole life. He rubbed his eyes, thinking he must be dreaming, and looked and looked again. There sure enough was a tiny man, no bigger than one foot five inches high, sitting gracefully on a round straw mat.

Filled with wonder, Tametomo walked to the edge of the sand, and as the little creature floated nearer on an incoming wave he said: "Who are you?"

"I am the bearer of small-pox," answered the stranger pigmy.

"And why, may I ask, do you come to this island?" inquired Tametomo.

"I have never been here before, so I came partly for sight-seeing and partly with the desire to seize hold of the inhabitants," answered the little creature.

Before he could finish his sentence Tametomo said angrily: "You spirit of hateful pestilence! Silence, I say! I am no other than Chinsei Hachirō Tametomo! Get out of my presence at once and take yourself far from this place, or I will make you repent the day you ever came here!"

As Tametomo spoke, the pigmy shrank and shrank from the form of a tiny man one foot five inches high, till only something the size of a pea was left in the middle of the straw mat. As he dwindled and dwindled, the little creature said that he was sorry that he had intruded into the island, but he had not known that it was in Tametomo's possession. And then he floated away out to sea on his straw mat as quickly and mysteriously as he had come.

The island of Oshima has always been free from small-pox, and to this day the islanders ascribe the immunity they enjoy from the horrible pestilence to Tametomo, who drove away the pigmy when the hateful creature would have landed there.

A Fleet

Now that Tametomo had subdued the demons on the neighboring island and had driven away the spirit of small-pox from Oshima, he was looked upon as a king by the simple islanders. They rendered him every possible honor and bowed their heads in the dust before him whenever he went abroad.

At last this state of affairs was reported to the authorities in the capital. The ministers of state decided that it was unsafe to allow this to go on. Such a popular and powerful hero was a menace to the Bakufu. Tametomo, the champion archer, must be put down and without delay. Such was the decree. A messenger was then and there despatched with sealed orders to general Shigemitsu, in the province of Izu, to set sail with his men for Oshima and subdue Tametomo.

One day Tametomo was standing on the beach and watching with pleasure, as he often did, the ever-whispering sea laughing and sparkling in the sunshine, when he saw fifty war-junks coming towards the island. The warriors standing on the fifty decks were all armed with swords and bows and arrows, and clad in armour from head to foot, and they were beating drums

Tametomo and his people spot the punitive fleet

and singing martial songs. Tametomo smiled when he saw this fleet all mustered in martial array and sent against him, a single man, for he knew, somehow or other, what they had come for.

"Now," he said proudly to himself, "the opportunity is given me of trying my archer's skill once more." Seizing his bow, he pulled it to the shape of a full moon, and aiming it at the foremost ship, sent an arrow right into the prow. In an instant the boat was upset and the warriors pitched into the sea.

Till that moment Tametomo had feared that his arm had lost its first great strength, since his enemies had cut the sinews. But on the contrary he now found that not only were his arms as strong as ever, but had even grown longer, and that he was able to pull his bow wider than before. He clapped his hands with joy at the discovery and called aloud: "This is a happy thing!"

But now Tametomo reflected that if he fought against those who had been sent by the Bakufu to take him, he would only bring trouble on the people of the island, who had been so kind to him and who had sheltered him in his exile. He thought of how in their simple reverence for his great strength they had almost worshipped him as a deified hero and had looked up to him as their leader. No—he would not, could not, bring war and trouble and certain punishment upon these good folk.

And thus he escaped from Oshima and reached Sanuki. Here he visited the late emperor's tomb and offered up prayers for the illustrious dead. Believing that his day of usefulness was over, he prepared to kill himself. Then, suddenly, as in a dream, Emperor Yorinaga, his father, and all those royalists who had fought and died in the civil war, or had been taken prisoners and killed by the victorious parties of the new emperor, appeared to him in the clouds and with a warning gesture prevented him from committing the dread deed of *harakiri*. As Tametomo gazed wonderingly at the beautiful vision, the bamboo curtain which hung before the ex-emperor's palanquin lifted, and as the sunshine and grace of His Majesty's smile fell upon the awe-stricken man, the sword dropped from his hand and the wish to die expired in his breast. He fell forward in humble prostration to the ground. When Tametomo lifted his head, the vision had vanished within the clouds; nothing remained to be seen of the royal array which had saved him from his self-imposed death.

This wonderful visitation changed Tametomo's mind. He gave up all idea of seeking death, and, leaving Sanuki, journeyed to Kyushu, and took up his abode on Mount Kihara. Here he collected a band of followers, and with them embarked on board a ship with the intention of reaching the capital

Tametomo is shipwrecked off the Ryūkyū islands

and once more striking a blow at the arrogant and usurping House of Taira. But misfortune followed him. He was overtaken by a storm, his ship was wrecked, his men lost, while he only narrowly escaped with his life to the island of Ryūkyū. Here he found the people in a state of great excitement, for a party of rebels had risen against the king, who was greatly oppressed by them, Tametomo put himself at the head of the loyalists, rescued the king, who had been taken prisoner, subdued the rebels, and then restored peace to the disturbed islands. For these meritorious services the king adopted him as his son, bestowed upon him the title of Prince, and married him to one of the royal princesses.

At last one day, when Tametomo had reached a good old age, happy in the life of peace and bliss with which his later years had been crowned, as he was walking along one of the spacious verandas of the palace, his attendants noticed a trail of cloud coming towards their master from the sky. As soon as the cloud touched Tametomo, he began to rise in the air before their astonished gaze. Lost in speechless amazement, they watched the hero mount higher and higher, till the clouds closed round him and hid him from their view. Such is the pretty legend of the earthly end of the brave archer Tametomo, one of the most interesting figures in Japanese history, who conquered the trials and misfortunes of his youth, and won through to bright days of prosperity. He left a son called Shunten, who became king of Ryūkyū in due time.

MINAMOTO YOSHITSUNE

Tokiwa Gozen

In old Japan more than seven hundred years ago a fierce war raged between the two great clans, the Taira and the Minamoto. These two famous clans were always contesting together for political power and military supremacy, and the country was torn in two with the many bitter battles that were fought. Indeed it may be said that the history of Japan for many years was the history of these two mighty martial families. Sometimes the Minamoto and sometimes the Taira gained victory, or were beaten. But their swords knew no rest for a period of many years. At last a strong and valiant general arose in the house of Minamoto. His name was Yoshitomo. At this time there were two aspirants for the imperial throne and civil war was raging in the capital. One imperial candidate was supported by the Taira, the other by the Minamoto. Yoshitomo, though a Minamoto, sided at first with the Taira against the reigning emperor. But when he saw how cruel and relentless their chieftain, Kiyomori, was, he turned against him and called all his followers to rally round the Minamoto standard and fight to put down the Taira.

But fate was against the gallant and doughty warrior Yoshitomo, and he suffered a crushing defeat at the hands of the Taira. He and his men, while fleeing from the vigilance of their enemies, were overtaken within the city gates, and ruthlessly slaughtered by Kiyomori and his warriors.

Yoshitomo left behind him his beautiful young wife, Tokiwa Gozen, and eight children, to mourn his untimely death. Five of the elder children were

by a first wife. The third of these became Yoritomo, the great first *shōgun* of Japan, while the eighth and youngest child was Ushiwaka, about whom this story is written. Ushiwaka and the hero Yoshitsune were one and the same person. Ushiwaka (Young Ox—he was so called because of his wonderful strength) was his name as a boy, and Yoshitsune was the name he took when he became of age.

At the time of his father's death, Ushiwaka was a babe in the arms of his mother, Tokiwa Gozen, but his tender age would not have saved his life had he been found by his father's enemies.

After the defeat they had inflicted on the rival clan, the Taira were all-powerful for a time. The Minamoto clan were in dire straits and in danger of being exterminated now, for so fierce was Kiyomori's hatred against his enemies that when a Minamoto fell into his cruel hands he immediately put the captive to death.

Realizing the great peril of the situation, Tokiwa Gozen, the widow of Yoshitomo, full of fear and anxiety for the safety of her little ones, quietly hid herself in the country, taking with her Ushiwaka and her two other children. So successful was Tokiwa Gozen in concealing her hiding-place that, though the Taira clan either killed or banished to a far-away island all the elder sons, relations, and partisans of the Minamoto chieftain, they could not discover the whereabouts of the mother and her children, notwithstanding the strict search Kiyomori had made.

Determined to have his will, and angry at being thwarted by a woman, Kiyomori at last hit on a plan which he felt sure would not fail to draw the wife of Yoshitomo from her hiding-place. He gave orders that Sekiya, the mother of the fair Tokiwa, should be seized and brought before him. He told her sternly that if she would reveal her daughter's hiding-place she should be well treated, but if she refused to do as she was told she would be tortured and put to death. When the old lady declared that she did not know where Tokiwa was, as in truth she did not, Kiyomori thrust her into prison and had her treated cruelly day after day.

Now the reason why Kiyomori was so set on finding Tokiwa and her sons was that while Yoshitomo's heirs lived he and his family could know no safety, for the strongest moral law in every Japanese heart was the old command, "A man may not live under the same heaven with the murderer of his father," and the Japanese warrior reckons nothing of life or death, of home or love in obeying this—as he deemed—supreme commandment. Women too burned with the same zeal in avenging the wrongs of their fathers and husbands.

Tokiwa Gozen, though hiding in the country, heard of what had befallen her mother, and great was her sorrow and distress. She sat down on the mats and moaned aloud: "It is wrong of me to let my poor innocent mother suffer to save myself and my children, but if I give myself up, Kiyomori will surely take my lord's sons and kill them.—What shall I do? Oh! what shall I do?"

Tokiwa Gozen
bemoans her fate

Poor Tokiwa! Her heart was torn between her love for her mother and her love for her children. Her anxiety and distraction were pitiful to see. Finally she decided that it was impossible for her to remain silent under the circumstances; she could not endure the thought that her mother was suffering persecution while she had the power of preventing it. And thus, holding the infant Ushiwaka in her bosom under her *kimono*, she took his two elder brothers (one seven and the other five years of age) by the hand and started for the capital.

In those days all travelling by ordinary people had to be done on foot. *Daimyōs* and great and important personages were carried in palanquins, and only they could travel in comfort and in state. Tokiwa could not hope to meet with kindness or hospitality on the way, for she was a Minamoto, and the Taira being all-powerful it was death to any one to harbour a Minamoto fugitive. So the obstacles that beset Tokiwa were great. But she was a samurai woman, and she quailed not at duty, however hard or stern that duty was. The greater the difficulties, the higher her courage rose to meet them. At last she set out on her momentous and celebrated journey.

It was winter-time and snow lay on the ground, and the wind blew piercingly cold and the roads were bad. What Tokiwa, a delicately nurtured woman, suffered from cold and fatigue, from loneliness and fear, from anxiety for her little children, from dread lest she should reach the capital too late to save her old mother, who might die under the cruel treatment to which she was being subjected, or be put to death by Kiyomori, in his wrath, or finally lest she herself should be seized by the Taira, and her filial plan be frustrated before she could reach the capital—all this must have been greater than any words can tell.

Sometimes poor distressed Tokiwa sat down by the wayside to hush the wailing babe she carried in her bosom, or to rest the two little boys, who, tired and faint and famished, clung to her robes, crying for their usual rice. On and on she went, soothing and consoling them as best she could, till at last she reached Kyoto, weary, footsore, and almost heartbroken. But though she was almost overcome with exhaustion, yet her purpose never flagged. She went at once to the enemy's camp and asked to be admitted to the presence of general Kiyomori.

When she was shown into the dread man's presence, she prostrated herself at his feet and said that she had come to give herself up and to release her mother.

"I am Tokiwa—the widow of Yoshitomo. I have come with my three children to beseech you to spare my mother's life and to set her free. My poor old mother has done nothing wrong. I am guilty of hiding myself and the little ones, yet I pray humbly for your august forgiveness."

She pleaded in such an agonizing way that Kiyomori, the Taira chieftain, was struck with admiration for her filial piety, a virtue more highly esteemed than any other in Japan. He felt sincerely sorry for Tokiwa in her woe, and her beauty and her tears melted his hard heart, and he promised her that if she would become his wife he would spare not only her mother's life, but her three children also.

For the sake of saving her children's lives the sad-hearted woman consented to Kiyomori's proposal. It must have been terrible to her to wed with her lord's enemy, the very man who had caused his death. But the thought that by so doing she saved the lives of his sons, who would one day surely arise to avenge their father's cruel death, must have been her consolation and her recompense for the sacrifice.

Kiyomori showed himself kinder to Tokiwa than he had ever shown himself to any one, for he allowed her to keep the babe Ushiwaka by her side. The two elder boys he sent to a temple to be trained as monks under the tutelage of priests.

By placing them out of the world in the seclusion of priesthood, Kiyomori felt that he would have little to fear from them when they attained manhood. How terribly and bitterly he was mistaken!

Ushiwaka

Time passed by, and when the little babe Ushiwaka at last reached the age of seven, Kiyomori likewise took him from his mother and sent him to the priests. The sorrow of Tokiwa, bereft of the last child of her beloved lord Yoshitomo, can better be imagined than described. But in her golden cap-

tivity even Kiyomori had not been able to deprive her of one iota of the incomparable power of motherhood, that of influencing the life of her child to the end of his days. As the little fellow had lain in her arms night and day, as she crooned him to sleep and taught him to walk, she forever whispered the name of Minamoto Yoshitomo in his ear.

At last one day her patience was rewarded and Ushiwaka lisped his father's name correctly. Then Tokiwa clasped him proudly to her breast, and wept tears of thankfulness and joy and of sorrowing remembrance, for she could never even for a day banish Yoshitomo from her mind. As Ushiwaka grew older and could understand better what she said, Tokiwa would daily whisper, "Remember thy father, Minamoto Yoshitomo! Grow strong and avenge his death, for he died at the hands of the Taira!" And day by day she told him stories of his great and good father—of his martial prowess in battle, and of his great strength and wonderful wielding of the sword, and she bade her little son remember and be like his father. And the mother's words and tears, sown in long years of patience and bitter endurance, bore fruit beyond all she had ever hoped or dreamed.

So Ushiwaka was taken from his mother at the age of seven, and was sent to the Tokobo monastery, at Kuramayama, to be trained as a monk.

Even at that early age he showed great intelligence, read the Sacred Books with avidity, and surprised the priests by his diligence and quickness of memory. He was naturally a very high-spirited youth, and could brook no control and hated to yield to others in anything whatsoever. As the years passed by and he grew older, he came to hear from his teachers and school friends of how his father Yoshitomo and his clan the Minamoto had been overthrown by the Taira, and this filled him with such intense sorrow and bitterness that sleeping or waking he could not banish the subject from his mind. As he listened daily to these things the words of his mother, which she had whispered in his ear as a child, now came throbbing back to his mind, and he understood their full meaning for the first time. In the lonely nights he felt again her hot tears falling on his face, and heard her repeat as clearly as a bell in the silence of the darkness: "Remember thy father, Minamoto Yoshitomo! Avenge his death, for he died at the hands of the Taira!"

Opposite page: the young Ushiwaka

At last one night the lad dreamed that his mother, beautiful and sad as he remembered her in the days of his childhood, came to his bedside and said to him, while the tears streamed down her face: "Avenge thy father, Yoshitomo! Unless thou remember my last words, I cannot rest in my grave. I am dying, Ushiwaka, remember!"

And Ushiwaka awoke as he cried aloud in his agony: "I will! Honorable mother, I will!" From that night his heart burned within him and the fire and love of clan-race stirred his soul. Continual brooding over the wrongs of his clan generated in his heart a fierce desire for revenge, and he finally resolved to abandon the priesthood, become a great general like his father, and punish the Taira. And as his ambition was fired and exalted and his mind thrilled back to the days when his poor unhappy mother Tokiwa prayed and wept over him, daily whispering in his ear the name of his father, his will grew to purpose strong. Tokiwa had not suffered in vain. From this time on, Ushiwaka bided his time every night till all in the monastery were fast asleep. When he heard the priests snoring, and knew himself safe from observation, he would steal out from the monastery, and, making his way down the hillside into the valley, he would draw his wooden sword and practise fencing by himself, and, striking the trees and the stones imagine that they were his Taira foes. As he worked in this way night after night, he felt his muscles grow strong, and this practice taught him how to wield his sword with skill.

One night as usual Ushiwaka had gone out to the valley and was diligently brandishing about his wooden sword. His mind fully bent upon his self-taught lesson, he was marching up and down, chanting snatches of war-songs and striking the trees and the rocks, when suddenly a great cloud spread over the heavens, the rain fell, the thunder roared, and the lightning flashed, and a great noise went through the valley, as if all the trees were being torn up by their roots and their trunks were splitting.

While Ushiwaka wondered what this could mean, a great giant over ten feet in height stood before him. He had large round glaring eyes that glinted like metal mirrors. His nose was bright red, and it must have been about a foot long. His hands were like the claws of a bird, and to each there were only two fingers. The feathers of long wings at each side peeped from under the creature's robes, and he looked like a gigantic goblin. Fearful indeed was

this apparition. But Ushiwaka was a brave and spirited youth and the son
of a warrior, and he was not to be daunted by anything. Without moving a
muscle of his face he gripped his sword more tightly and simply asked:
"Who are you, sir?"

The goblin laughed aloud and said: "I am the king of the *tengu*, the elves
of the mountains, and I have made this valley my home for many a long year.
I have admired your perseverance in coming to this place night after night
for the purpose of practising fencing all by yourself, and I have come to meet
you, with the intention of teaching you all I know of the art of the sword."

Ushiwaka was delighted when he heard this, for the *tengu* have supernatural powers, and fortunate indeed are those whom they favor. He
thanked the giant elf and expressed his readiness to begin at once. He then
drew his sword and began to attack the king of the *tengu*, but the king
shifted his position with the quickness of lightning, and taking from his
belt a fan made of seven feathers parried the showering blows right and
left so cleverly that the young warrior's interest became thoroughly
aroused. Every night he came out for the lesson. He never missed once,
summer or winter, and in this way he learned all the secrets of the art
which the king of the *tengu* could teach him.

Ushiwaka meets the
king of the *tengu*

The *tengu* king was a great master and Ushiwaka an apt pupil. He became so proficient in fencing that he could overcome ten or twenty small *tengu* in the twinkling of an eye, and he acquired extraordinary skill and dexterity in the use of the sword. And the *tengu* also imparted to him the wonderful adroitness and agility which made him so famous in after-life.

Musashibō Benkei

Now Ushiwaka was about fifteen years old, a comely youth, and tall for his age. At this time there lived on Mount Hiei, just outside the capital, a wild monk named Musashibō Benkei, who was such a lawless and turbulent fellow that he had become notorious for his deeds of violence. The city rang with the stories of his misdeeds, and so well known had he become that people could not hear his name without fear and trembling.

Benkei suddenly made up his mind that it would be good sport to steal a thousand swords from various warriors.

No sooner did the wild idea enter his head than he began to put it into practice. Every night he sauntered forth to the Gojō bridge of Kyoto, and when a warrior or any man carrying a sword passed by, Benkei would snatch the weapon from his girdle. If the owners yielded up their blades quietly, Benkei allowed them to pass unhurt, but if not, he would strike them dead with a single blow of the huge halberd he carried. So great was Benkei's strength that he always overcame his victim,—resistance was useless,—and night by night one and sometimes two men met their death at his hands on the Gojō bridge. In this way Benkei gained such a terrible reputation that everybody far and near feared to meet him, and after dark no one dared to pass the bridge he was known to haunt, so fearful were the tales told of the dreaded robber of swords.

At last this story reached the ears of Ushiwaka, and he said to himself: "What an interesting man this must be! If it is true that he is a monk, he must be a strange one indeed. But as he only robs people of their swords, he cannot be a common highwayman. If I could make such a strong man a retainer of mine, he would be of great assistance to me when I punish my

enemies, the Taira clan. Good! To-night I will go to the Gojō bridge and try the mettle of this Benkei!"

Ushiwaka, being a youth of great courage, had no sooner made up his mind to meet Benkei than he proceeded to put his plan into execution. He started out that same evening. It was a beautiful moonlit night, and taking with him his favorite flute he strolled forth through the streets of the sleeping city till he came to the Gojō bridge. Then from the opposite direction came a tall figure which appeared to touch the clouds, so gigantic was its stature. The stranger was clad in a suit of coal-black armour and carried an immense halberd.

"This must be the sword-robber! He is indeed strong!" said Ushiwaka to himself, but he was not in the least daunted, and went on playing his flute quite calmly.

Presently the giant halted and gazed at Ushiwaka, but evidently thought him a mere youth, and decided to let him go unmolested, for he was about to pass him by without lifting a hand. This indifference on the part of Benkei not only disappointed but angered Ushiwaka. Having waited in vain for the stranger to offer violence, our hero approached Benkei, and, with the intention of picking a quarrel, suddenly kicked the latter's halberd out of his hand.

Ushiwaka encounters
the monk Benkei on
Gojō bridge

Benkei, who had first thought to spare Ushiwaka on account of his youth, became very angry when he found himself insulted by a lad to whom he had been intentionally kind. In a fury he exclaimed, "Miserable stripling!" and raising his halberd struck sideways at Ushiwaka, thinking to slice him in two at the waist and to see his body fall asunder. But the young warrior nimbly avoided the blow which would have killed him, and springing back a few paces he flung his *tessen* (iron battle fan) at Benkei's head and uttered a loud cry of defiance. The fan struck Benkei on the forehead right between the eyes, making him mad with pain. In a transport of rage Benkei aimed a fearful blow at Ushiwaka, as if he were splitting a log of wood with an axe. This time Ushiwaka sprang up to the parapet of the bridge, clapped his hands, and laughed in derision, saying:

"Here I am! Don't you see? Here I am!" and Benkei was again thwarted thus.

Benkei, who had never known his strokes miss before, had now failed twice in catching this nimble opponent. Frantic with chagrin and baffled rage, he now rushed furiously to the attack, whirling his great halberd round in all directions till it looked like a water-wheel in motion, striking wildly

Ushiwaka evades
Benkei's attacks

and blindly at Ushiwaka. But the young warrior had been taught tricks innumerable by the giant *tengu* of Kuramayama, and he had profited so well by his lessons that the king of the *tengu* had at last said that even he could teach him nothing more, and now, as it may well be imagined, he was too quick for the heavy Benkei. When Benkei struck in front, Ushiwaka was behind, and when Benkei aimed a blow behind, Ushiwaka darted in front. Nimble as a monkey and swift as a swallow, Ushiwaka avoided all the blows aimed at him, and, finding himself outmatched, even the redoubtable Benkei grew tired.

Ushiwaka saw that Benkei was played out. He kept up the game a little longer and then changed his tactics. Seizing his opportunity, he knocked Benkei's halberd out of his hand. When the giant stooped to pick his weapon up, Ushiwaka ran behind him and with a quick movement tripped him up. There lay the big man on all fours, while Ushiwaka nimbly strode across his back and pressing him down asked him how he liked this kind of play.

All this time Benkei had wondered at the courage of the youth in attacking and challenging a man so much larger than himself, but now he was filled with amazement at Ushiwaka's wonderful strength and adroitness.

"I am indeed astonished at what you have done," said Benkei. "Who in the world can you be? I have fought with many men on this bridge, but you are the first of my antagonists who has displayed such strength. Are you a god or a *tengu*? You certainly cannot be an ordinary human being!"

Ushiwaka laughed and said: "Are you afraid for the first time, then?"

"I am," answered Benkei.

"Will you from henceforth be my retainer?" demanded Ushiwaka.

"I will in very truth be your retainer, but may I know who you are?" asked Benkei meekly.

Ushiwaka now felt sure that Benkei was in earnest. He therefore allowed him to get up from the ground, and then said: "I have nothing to hide from you. I am the youngest son of Minamoto Yoshitomo and my name is Ushiwaka."

Benkei started with surprise when he heard these words and said: "What is this I hear? Are you in truth a son of the lord Yoshitomo of the Minamoto clan? That is the reason I felt from the first moment of our encounter that

藤原秀郷龍宮城
蜈蚣城射玉之圖

your deeds were not those of a common person. No wonder that I thought this! I am only too happy to become the retainer of such a distinguished and spirited young warrior. I will follow you as my lord and master from this moment onward, if you will allow me. I can wish for no greater honor."

So there and then, on the Gojō bridge in the silver moonlight, the monk Benkei vowed to be the true and faithful vassal of the young warrior Ushiwaka and to serve him loyally till death, and thus was the compact between lord and vassal made. From that time on, Benkei gave up his wild and lawless ways and devoted his life to the service of Ushiwaka, who was highly pleased at having won such a strong liegeman to his side.

Meeting His Brother

Although Ushiwaka had now secured Benkei, it was impossible for only two men, however strong, to think of fighting the Taira clan, so they both decided that the cherished plan must wait till the Minamoto were stronger. While thus waiting they heard a report that a descendant of Tawara no Tōda Hidesato named Fujiwara Hidehira was now a famous general in Kaiwai of the Ashu province, and that he was so powerful that no one dared oppose him. Hearing this, Ushiwaka thought that it would be a good plan to pay the general a visit and try to interest him, if possible, in the fortunes of the House of Minamoto. He consulted with Benkei, who encouraged the young warrior in his scheme of enlisting the general Hidehira as a partisan, and the two therefore left Kyoto secretly and journeyed as quickly as possible to Oshu on this errand.

On the way there, Ushiwaka and Benkei came to the temple of Atsuta, and as they considered it important that the young warrior should look older now, Ushiwaka performed the ceremony of *genpuku* at the shrine. This was a rite performed in olden times when youths reached the age of manhood, They then had to shave off the front part of their hair and to change their names as a sign that they had left childhood behind. Ushiwaka now took the name of Yoshitsune. As he was the eighth son, it would have been more correct for him to have assumed the name of Hachirō, but as his uncle Tametomo the

Opposite page:
Tawara no Tōda
Hidesato, founder of
the Fujiwara clan

Archer, of whom you have already read, was named Hachirō, he purposely did not take this name. From this time forth our hero is known as Yoshitsune, and this name he has glorified forever by his wonderful bravery and many heroic exploits. In Japanese history he is the warrior without fear and without reproach, the darling of the people, to them almost an incarnation of Hachiman, the popular God of War. And as for Benkei, never can you find in all history a vassal who was more true or loyal to his master than Benkei. He was Yoshitsune's right hand in everything, and his strength and wisdom carried them successfully through many a dire emergency.

From Kyoto to Oshu is a long journey of about three hundred miles, but at length Yoshitsune (as we must now call him) and Benkei reached their destination and craved the general Hidehira's assistance. They found that Hidehira was a warm adherent of the Minamoto cause, and under the late lord Yoshitomo he and his family had enjoyed great favor. When the general learned, therefore, that Yoshitsune was the son of the illustrious Minamoto chieftain, his joy knew no bounds, and he made Yoshitsune and Benkei heartily welcome and treated them both as guests of honor and importance.

Just at this time Yoshitsune's eldest brother, Yoritomo, who had been banished to an island in the province of Izu, collected a great army and raised his standard against the Taira. When the news about Yoritomo reached Yoshitsune, he rejoiced, for he felt that the hour had at last come when the Minamoto would be revenged on the Taira for all the wrongs they had suffered at the hands of the latter.

With the help of Hidehira and the faithful Benkei, he collected a small army of warriors and at once marched over to his brother's camp in Izu. He sent a messenger ahead to inform Yoritomo that his youngest brother, now named Yoshitsune, was coming to aid him in his fight against the Taira.

Yoritomo was exceedingly glad at this unexpected good news, for all that helped to swell his forces now brought nearer the day when he would be able to strike his long-planned blow at the power of the hated Taira. As soon as Yoshitsune reached Izu, Yoritomo arranged for an immediate meeting. Although the two men were brothers, it must be remembered that their father had been killed, and the family utterly scattered, when they were mere children, Yoshitsune being at that time but an infant in his mother's arms. As this was therefore the first time they had met Yoritomo knew nothing of his young brother's character.

One of Yoshitsune's elder brothers had come with him, and Yoritomo being a shrewd general wished to test them both to see of what mettle they were made. He ordered his retainers to bring a brass basin full of boiling water. When it was brought, Yoritomo ordered Noriyori, the elder of the two, to carry it to him first. Now brass being a good conductor of heat, the basin was very hot and Noriyori stupidly let it fall. Yoritomo ordered it to be filled again and bade Yoshitsune bring it to him. Without moving a muscle of his handsome face Yoshitsune took hold of the almost unbearably hot vessel and carried it with due ceremony slowly across the room. This exhibition of nerve and endurance filled Yoritomo with admiration and he was favorably struck with Yoshitsune's character. As for Noriyori, who had been unable to hold a hot basin for a few moments, he had no use for him at all, except as a common warrior.

Yoritomo begged Yoshitsune to become his right-hand man and zealously to espouse his cause. Yoshitsune declared that this had been his lifelong ambition ever since he could remember, as they both were sons of the same father, so was their cause and destiny one. Yoritomo made Yoshitsune

Yoshitsune (center) comes face to face with his older brother (right)

a general of part of his army and ordered him in the name of his father Yoshitomo to chastise the Taira.

Delighted beyond all words at the wonderfully auspicious turn events were taking, Yoshitsune hastened his preparations for the march. The longed-for hour had come to which through his whole childhood and youth he had looked forward, and for which his whole being had thirsted for many years. He could now fulfil the last words of his unhappy mother, and punish the Taira for all the evil they had wrought against the Minamoto. All the wild restlessness of his youth, which had driven him forth to wield his wooden sword against the rocks in the Kuramayama Valley and to try his strength against Benkei on the Gojō bridge, now found vent in action most dear to a born warrior's heart. With several thousands of troops under him, Yoshitsune marched up to Kyoto and waged war against the Taira, and defeated them in a series of brilliant engagements.

The stricken Taira multitudes fled before the avenger like autumn leaves before the blast, and Yoshitsune pursued them to the sea. At Dan no Ura the Taira made a last stand, but all in vain. Their lion leader, Kiyomori, was dead, and there was no great chieftain to rally them in the disordered retreat that now ensued. Yoshitsune came sweeping down upon them, and they and

Fighting the Taira in the snow

their fleet and their infant emperor likewise, with their women and children, sank beneath the waves. Only a scattered few lived to tell the tale of the terrible destruction that overtook them on the sea.

Thus did Yoshitsune become a great warrior and general. Thus did he fulfil the ambitions of his youth and avenge his father Yoshitomo's death. He was without a rival in the whole country for his marvellous bravery and successive victories. He was adored by the people as their most popular hero and darling, and throughout the length and breadth of the land his praise was sung by everyone.

Fighting the Taira at
Dan no Ura

MUSASHIBÔ BENKEI

Oniwaka

Those who have read the story of the great warrior Yoshitsune will certainly remember that his retainer Benkei was a gigantic monk as remarkable for his physical strength as he was for his original character. In the story of Yoshitsune very little was said about Benkei. You may therefore like to hear something more about the famous man who is so favorite a hero with Japanese children and so greatly respected in Japan for his faithfulness to his master.

Benkei was the son of a Buddhist priest named Benshō, High Steward of the temple of Gongen at Kumano, a famous shrine from ancient times, and his mother was the daughter of a high court official of the second rank.

Benkei was no ordinary mortal. Most children come into the world within ten months, but Benkei kept his mother waiting one year and six months for him. And when he was born he already had teeth and a luxuriant growth of hair, and was so strong and big that he could walk from the first as well as most children of two or three years of age.

Seeing how extraordinarily big and strong he was, the family were lost in amazement. But their wonder quickly changed to dismay, for the mother died soon after giving birth to her son. The father, Benshō, was very angry at this, and took an aversion to the child who had brought, he said, so great a misfortune upon him. He even wished to abandon the boy altogether, believing that, as Benkei's birth had cost his mother's life, he would in after years only prove a curse to the family.

Now the boy's aunt (who was married to a man named Yama no I), hearing this, pitied her little nephew Benkei, and going to her brother said: "If you are going to treat the child so cruelly as to cast him away, please give him to me. I have no children and will bring him up as my own child. He is not responsible for his mother's death. It is fate, and there is no help for it!"

Benshō consented to her taking the child, saying that he did not care what happened to him so long as he was kept out of his sight, for he could no longer bear to see him. So Benkei was adopted by his aunt, who took him away to the capital of Kyoto.

The child rewarded her care and grew to be a fine boy beyond all expectation. He was exceedingly strong and healthy. At five or six years of age he was equal in size and strength to boys of ten or twelve, and gave promise of unusual intelligence and cleverness.

Unfortunately his face was as fierce as that of a demon and he looked so truly savage and ugly that he gradually earned for himself the nickname of Oniwaka, or Demon Youth.

In a few years his uncle thought that it was time to send the boy to school, and he accordingly sent Benkei to the monastery of Eizan and placed him under the tutorship of the famous priest Kankei. In Japan in those times all learning was in the hands of the priests, and the temples were the only schools.

When Benkei arrived at Kankei's temple he was taught the reading and writing of Chinese characters, and as he was at first docile and diligent, and obedient to all set over him, he made rapid progress, and not only satisfied but pleased his teacher, who commended his industry. But after a time he chafed at the restraint of his new surroundings and began to give trouble. Not content with being unruly himself, he would lead the other novices away from their studies into the mountains and play all kinds of rough games with them, and, of course, being by nature much stronger and bigger than any of them, none of his companions could stand against him. It therefore happened that in every contest he invariably gained the victory, and this elated him so much that he thought of nothing but his sports and his triumphs, and, neglecting his lessons entirely, practised athletic games day after day, quite forgetting everything else.

Oniwaka's teacher, Kankei, hearing about the youth's wild doings, and considering them as unseemly, sent for him and told him that such behavior not only grieved his guardians but brought disgrace upon the holy temple. But his rebuke fell upon deaf ears and did no good at all. While he was being scolded, Benkei listened respectfully enough. But as soon as the reverend teacher turned his back he would forthwith be as wild, if not wilder, than ever. His conduct grew worse and worse, till at last, losing all patience, the master priest forbade him to go out of the house, and then enforced his order by shutting him up in a monastery.

This punishment Oniwaka deeply resented, and one night, eluding the vigilance of his gaolers, he stole out quietly, and picking up a great log of wood began to destroy everything he could. First he smashed the gateway, then the fences all round the temple, then he broke the shutters and the sliding screens inside. Indeed everything he could reach, he wrecked. The monks, roused from their slumbers by the unexpected noise, which sounded as if a troop of robbers were at work, were all so frightened that they could do nothing to stop the whirlwind of destruction. When Oniwaka had done all the mischief he could he felt that, after this last mad prank, the temple of Eizan was no place for him, so he fled from the spot forever. He was now just seventeen years of age, and he called himself Musashibō Benkei.

Oniwaka showed a sense of humor when he called himself Musashibō Benkei. In olden times there lived in Eizan a man named Musashi, who was turbulent and wild in his youth, and yet became a famous monk and lived until the ripe age of sixty-one. Oniwaka, having heard about this famous man, made up his mind to be like him, and therefore called himself Musashibō, or Musashi the Bonze. The first syllable *ben* of Benkei was taken from the first character of his father's name, Benshō, and the second, *kei*, was the last syllable of his teacher, Kankei. The name Benkei was therefore a combination of the names of his father and teacher.

Ashamed to return home to his uncle and aunt after his behavior at the monastery, Benkei made up his mind to travel. This he did much after the fashion of German apprentices at about the same period in Europe. Leaving

The mighty Benkei drags a temple bell up the mountain

Kyoto, he came to Osaka. From Osaka he went to the province of Awa on the island of Shikoku. He then travelled all through that island, and thence wandered back to the mainland, where in the province of Harima he came at last to a monastery called Shosa. This monastery was as large as that of Eizan, and Benkei thought that he would like to stay there for a time as a student. With the consent of the abbot, Benkei was enrolled as a monk of this temple.

Among the numerous novices in the temple there was one named Kaien, who was nearly as fond of mischief as Benkei himself, and he was known in the neighborhood for a troublesome fellow, no one young or old being safe from his foolish pranks. One day soon after Benkei's arrival, Kaien found the newcomer taking a nap, so for fun he wrote on Benkei's cheek the Chinese character for *geta*, or "clog."

When Benkei woke up and went into the courtyard he noticed that everybody he came near seemed to be laughing at him, though nobody would say why.

Thinking that there must be something strange in his appearance he glanced into a bowl of water and at once discovered the cause of the merriment. Angry at the trick played on him, he seized a thick stick and rushing into the midst of his fellow novices shouted: "You rogues! I suppose you thought that you were doing something clever when you scribbled on my face. Now just come here, one by one, and kneel down and beg my pardon. If you do not you will soon be sorry for yourselves."

Benkei looked so angry and spoke so fiercely that most of the monks were frightened. Four or five of the boldest answered him back, saying: "What do you mean, you lazy fellow, by complaining about a trick played upon you while you were asleep in the middle of the day? If we hear any more of your grumbling, we will throw you out of the monastery."

In this way they tried to frighten Benkei, but he did not budge an inch, and his only reply was to lift his stick and knock down the four or five who had spoken.

Seeing this, Kaien, the author of all this trouble, rushed up, saying: "You are a coward to attack fellows half your size. Suppose for a change you fight with me!"

Then looking round for a weapon, and seeing a large log of wood on a fire close by, he picked it up and faced the enraged Benkei, adding: "It was I who scribbled on your face. If you are angry, come on and let us fight it out!"

The two closed at once and fought for some time. Then Benkei grew impatient, and seizing Kaien by his collar and belt lifted him off his feet. The other novices, seeing this, cried out in alarm: "Kaien has been lifted off his feet. He can't fight now. He is helpless!"

Then they shouted to Kaien to apologize and save himself.

"Pardon! Pardon! Benkei! Mercy!" screamed the youth, now bitterly repenting his folly.

Benkei did not hear Kaien's cry for mercy, for he was like a madman now. He hardly knew what he did or said, for his blood was fired by the taunts of the young men and by the fight.

"You shall die," screamed Benkei, "mannerless coward that you are. You shall die, I say, and your carcass shall be eaten by crows!" With these words he shook Kaien as mercilessly as a dog does a rat, and then flung him upon the tiled roof of the chapel, a height of some fourteen or fifteen feet. Kaien fell on the roof, rolled down the tiles, and at last, striking a rock in the garden, was killed on the spot. When the foolish and unfortunate lad was flung up on the roof by Benkei, he still held the smoking brand which he had all to no purpose used against his antagonist and this, falling on the building, flared up and set fire to the temple. Just then a breeze sprang up and fanned the flames into a fierce blaze. Sparks from the roof dropped upon the curving tiers of the five-storied pagoda, and the main gateway, and the school and the houses of the monks, till the whole of the monastery was in a blaze. Seeing the conflagration, all the inmates were lost in consternation. Shouting "Fire! Fire!" some of them ran to draw water from the well, while others threw sand on the flames, and in the excitement and general confusion which followed, Benkei, the cause of the calamity, was forgotten.

In the midst of the tremendous tumult and disturbance Benkei laughed quietly to himself.

"Ha! ha!" he laughed, "look at the fire and the stir I have made! I have never seen the lazy monks know what it is to hurry before. It will do them good for once in a way!"

Then he slipped away from the temple and made his way back to Kyoto.

Benkei, wild and unruly as he was, cannot be judged by the standard of conduct of today. Those times were very different from these days of peace and order. Young men were encouraged to do rough violent deeds to show their strength and courage, and if they killed their antagonists in the fight, so much the more did this add to their credit. It was the custom for a young samurai on obtaining a sword to go out into the highways to try the mettle of his blade. Woe to those who passed by; their blood must baptize the warrior's sword. This training bred a martial spirit in the youth of Japan, and produced brave men of dauntless courage and resolution like Benkei, who became such a hero in after-life.

Finding His Master

Benkei was by this time tired of study and of living the dull life of a monk, and he now made up his mind to rove about in search of adventures, determining that, should he find a stronger man than himself, he would become that man's vassal, turn from his wild ways and lead the life of a good samurai, faithful to his lord and a good patriot to his country. But first of all he must find the man stronger than he to whom he would bow his proud strong neck. He longed now to find a master worthy of respect, whom he could reverence as his superior. How was this to be done? At last an idea struck him. He had determined to be a warrior and enter the service of a samurai. He must therefore get a good sword. Violent and impetuous as ever, to this end he now vowed to take a thousand swords from the citizens of Kyoto. To carry out his wild scheme he went nightly to the Gojō bridge, and when men passed along bearing swords in their girdles he would rush suddenly out, attack them furiously, and snatch away their swords. He never pursued those who ran away, for he deemed them cowards and would not waste his time or strength on such creatures. But those who opposed him he would mow down with a single sweep of his great halberd. In this way he attacked nine hundred and ninety-nine men and took away nine hundred and ninety-nine swords. Each time he had hoped to meet his match in the numerous contests, but not one among the whole number proved a serious foe.

Accordingly the swords Benkei thus collected were all poor weapons, for weak men have like swords. They were all blunt and badly tempered and of not the slightest use. He was heartily disappointed, and began to think that perhaps he had better abandon the enterprise as a vain one. In desperation he determined to get one more sword and thus complete the total of one thousand blades, the number he had first of all set his mind upon. In spite of discouragement, he told himself that it would be stupid to give up.

As soon as he had decided to do this, his spirits revived, and for some unaccountable reason he felt that this time he would be lucky, and able to secure once and for all a good weapon. He waited impatiently for the evening, and as soon as the twilight fell he made his preparations and went as usual to the Gojō bridge. It happened to be the night of the fifteenth day of August, and the beautiful harvest moon sailed up into the serene heaven, above the hills and the tall dark velvety pines and cryptomerias, and the sleeping world was bathed in her soft silvery brilliance. For a long time Benkei stood leaning against the parapet of the bridge, entranced by the fair scene spread out before him in the moonlight and apparently quite forgetful for the time being of his purpose. Suddenly the stillness of the beautiful night was broken by the sound of a flute. Benkei started from his reverie. The music drew nearer and nearer, and then he saw a slight figure approaching from the other end of the bridge. The newcomer wore a kind of white veil and high black-lacquered clogs, and was playing on his flute as he strolled along. Benkei watched the approaching stranger and saw at once that this was no ordinary passer-by.

At first he thought that this must be a woman, for the moonlight revealed a slender grace in walking and then on nearer view a face of extreme youth and aristocratic beauty. He could not find the heart to attack the mysterious and gentle unknown, and decided to let him or her pass unmolested. But while he was wondering who the person, so unlike all the others he had met on the bridge, could be, the supposed lady all of a sudden stepped up to Benkei and kicked the latter's halberd out of his hand.

Is this a woman?

"What are you doing?" shouted Benkei, in a rage when he had recovered from his astonishment. And recovering his halberd he pulled off what he supposed to be the lady's veil. To his surprise he found that the adventurous stranger was a handsome youth who might easily be mistaken for a girl, and then Benkei's eyes fell upon a splendid gold-mounted sword which the lad carried in his girdle. He said to himself that he had not waited so long in vain, that he was in luck this night to have such a bird come into his net. While these thoughts flashed through his mind, Benkei clutched at the sword, but the youth was far stronger than he looked, and the instant Benkei put forth his hand the young fellow flung a *tessen* in his face, saying: "How brave you think yourself, don't you?" and darted out of his reach.

This made Benkei more angry than ever, and with threatening exclamations he lifted his halberd to deal a smashing blow on the young warrior. But the lad was far too quick for Benkei and sprang about with the nimbleness of a monkey, and no matter how Benkei aimed his blows, they never reached their mark. Never had Benkei seen such agility and adroitness. Sometimes the youth appeared in front and sometimes behind, now on one side and again on the other, and as often as Benkei turned he would find that his opponent had shifted his position like lightning. At length Benkei grew tired and a sense of awe began to take hold of his mind, for he now felt that the youth must be a supernatural being, or a *tengu*, and no common mortal, and this feeling grew upon him so strongly that he began to lose heart. He knew now that he was no longer invincible as he had hitherto been. Then the lad, who had hitherto acted on the defensive, began to push his advantage, and, attacking Benkei in good earnest, beat down the latter's guard and disarmed him.

When the redoubtable Benkei, who had never yet been beaten by any one in his whole life, found himself thus ignominiously defeated, he was astonished beyond words, and there and then, kneeling down on the bridge, bowed low before the young man and humbly said: "Will you condescend to tell me whose son you are, and your name? Something tells me that you are no common man!"

The handsome youth laughed and replied: "I am the eighth and youngest son of Minamoto Yoshitomo, and my name is Minamoto Ushiwaka," and with these words he allowed Benkei to rise.

"What do I hear?" exclaimed Benkei. "Are you indeed the young warrior Minamoto Ushiwaka of whom I have heard so much? I felt from the first that you were a person of distinction. As for myself, I am simply Musashibō Benkei. For a long time I have been looking for a man stronger than myself, to whom I could look up as my master. I have led a wild life for a long time, but if you will take me into your service I will be a good and faithful vassal."

Betrayal

From this moment Benkei was a completely changed character. He gave up his wild ways and became obedient to his young master, who was the only one he had found a match for his imposing strength and will. He served his new lord with the utmost devotion, and fought bravely in every battle which Yoshitsune (Ushiwaka's name when he came of age) waged against the Taira clan at the famous battles of Ichi no Tani and Dan no Ura.

Yoshitsune won victory after victory, driving his Taira enemies to the sea, where they miserably perished at Dan no Ura, and it seemed to the wondering people that he must be the impersonation of Hachiman, the God of War.

So handsome and brave was he that they had never seen or heard of his like before, and throughout Japan everyone praised and loved him. Now Yoritomo, when he saw his brother's popularity, became jealous, and Kajiwara, one of his generals, who hated Yoshitsune because the young warrior had once openly reproved him for cowardice, seized the opportunity to poison Yoritomo's mind against his younger brother. He suggested that Yoshitsune's aim was to supplant Yoritomo in supreme authority. Sad to say, Yoritomo believed this wicked slander. Therefore, when Yoshitsune, covered with glory and honor, returned from the wars, bringing with him, as prisoners of war, Munemori, the Taira chieftain, and his son (Kiyomori was now dead), he found that Yoritomo had erected a barrier near Koshigoe, just outside Kamakura. Here he sent a guard to receive the prisoners, but on the ground that Yoshitsune was guilty of treachery, Yoritomo refused him entry into Kamakura. In vain did Yoshitsune protest against the unjust accusation. In vain, too, did he write a touching letter avowing his unaltered

love and devotion to Yoritomo. And in vain did he recount all the hardships endured on the campaigns which the young and chivalrous general had undertaken at the command of his brother. He was not believed, and ingratitude was the only reward he received for devotion to his brother's cause. At this crisis Yoshitsune found himself banished and every part of Japan rendered unsafe for his residence, for Yoritomo ordered him to be arrested. When this time of trouble came, Benkei was indefatigable in his efforts to guard Yoshitsune's person from danger. He followed him in his flight and exile and never left his master's side.

Yoshitsune now returned to Kyoto for a time. Soon after he arrived there Yoritomo sent a man named Tosabō Shōshun to assassinate Yoshitsune. This man, like Benkei, had formerly been a monk, and he gave out that he had come to visit the temples of the capital.

Shōshun knew very well what a shrewd and clever warrior Yoshitsune was, and he doubted his own ability to cope with the task he had undertaken. He therefore decided that he would wait until Yoshitsune was completely off his guard, and then make a sudden attack upon the house where he was staying. He told his followers of his plan and secretly prepared for the raid.

Yoshitsune soon learned of Shōshun's coming, for the people of Kyoto and its neighborhood, where he had lived as a boy, were devoted to him. The young general, knowing that Shōshun was in Yoritomo's service, regarded him with suspicion. He told Benkei of his fears, and Benkei at once volunteered to go and summon Shōshun to the house and question him.

Yoshitsune agreed to the plan, and Benkei immediately set off for Shōshun's house.

"Now, Shōshun," said he, "my Lord Yoshitsune desires to see you, so you are to come back with me at once!"

Benkei's manner was so fierce and determined that Shōshun felt alarmed and he therefore pretended to be ill. But Benkei was not to be balked in that stupid way, and shouting: "If you are not quick, I'll seize you and take you whether you will or not!" he grabbed Shōshun by his girdle and lifted him up as if he had been a child, tucked him under one arm, and, mounting his horse, carried him off.

There were several of Shōshun's retainers present at the interview, but they were all trembling with fear and did not dare to put forth a hand to help their master.

Benkei thus conducted Shōshun into the presence of Yoshitsune by force, and both master and vassal began to examine him strictly. But Shōshun was such an audacious rascal that, notwithstanding the fact that he had actually come from Yoritomo, hired as an assassin, he refused to confess anything. With great humility he feigned surprise at being suspected of entertaining designs against Yoshitsune's life, saying that he was but a poor monk in Yoritomo's service, and as Yoshitsune was his master's brother, he (Shōshun) regarded him as his lord also. Nothing else but a religious fast and retreat had called him to Kyoto!

Now Yoshitsune and Benkei had no actual proof of his guilt, so they allowed Shōshun to go free, first making him sign a document declaring that he was not a hired assassin. In truth neither of them believed the crafty man, but thought him too despicable an enemy to fear, and made up their minds that, if he and his gang planned a night assault, the party could be easily repulsed and put to flight. Shōshun on his part congratulated himself on his cleverness, returned home, armed his men, and made an attack on Yoshitsune's residence.

Yoshitsune that night, thinking that at any rate for some time he was quite safe from attack, made merry with all his men. Drinking amber-colored wine they sat up late, and when at last the young general retired to rest, having drunk much he slept a deep sleep. His beautiful young wife Shizuka, who accompanied him in all his wanderings, fearing she knew not what, that night alone kept watch beside her lord's couch. She was the first to hear the approach of Shōshun and his warriors. Vainly she tried to rouse Yoshitsune; she called him, she shook him, but all in vain,—he slept on. Shizuka was frantic. She heard the enemy at the gate trying to batter it down. Suddenly the thought struck her, as if by inspiration, that the most thrilling call to arms to a warrior must be the sound of his armour. She rushed to the box in the hall, and heavy as it was for her slender strength, she lifted out the armour. She dragged it quickly into the room. Then over Yoshitsune's head she waved it to and fro. "Clang-clang," sounded the armour, "clang—clang." Up sprang the warrior, seized the suit of armour, and with Shizuka's help dressed himself

for battle. All this took place without a single word. Benkei and the rest of his warriors soon joined him and the enemy were put to flight. Shōshun managed to escape and hide himself in the mountains of Kurama, near Kyoto, but he was caught and put to death at last.

To have been able to thwart and punish the assassins from Kamakura was a source of great satisfaction to Yoshitsune and his men. But when the story reached Yoritomo he was very angry, and issued another decree entirely disowning Yoshitsune and declaring him an enemy of the state.

Yoshitsune felt that Yoritomo was acting most unjustly towards him, for he knew himself to be entirely blameless of plotting against Yoritomo's supremacy. But as it was useless to contend against his elder brother, who as *shōgun* was the military ruler of Japan, he decided to leave Kyoto and escape to some other place. He therefore planned to cross from the province of Settsu to Saikoku in a ship. But when they reached Dan no Ura, where Yoshitsune had finally conquered and all but terminated the Taira clan, the fine weather they had hitherto experienced suddenly changed, the sky became overcast with black clouds, rain began to fall in torrents, the wind began to blow, and gradually the waves rose higher and higher, and shipwreck became

The beautiful Shizuka (left) helps to thwart Shōshun's night attack

111

Yoshitsune and his men sail for Dan no Ura

imminent. As the darkness deepened about them, though they could see nothing, over the water there came weird sounds of the din of battle, the rushing of ships through the sea, the shouting and trampling of men, the whizzing of arrows in the air. All around them as the ship sped on, the tumult of the fight grew louder, till Yoshitsune felt that he was living again through that awful and never-to-be-forgotten battle.

Then from amid the rolling waves, which every moment threatened to engulf the boat, arose pale, ghastly forms whose wan faces were terrible to see. Clad in blood-stained, battle-torn armour and ravaged with gaping wounds, these warrior ghosts raised threatening hands, as if to stop the progress of the boat, while meanings of despair and hollow sobs and shrieks burst from the spectre army. Among the foremost figures was one who brandished a huge halberd, and as he approached, he addressed Yoshitsune, saying: "Aha! Revenge! Revenge! Behold in me the ghost of Taira Tomomori, general of the Taira clan, ruthlessly destroyed by you! Long have I waited here for you and now I will slay you all, for not until then will the slaughtered Taira rest in their watery graves."

Through the tossing, whirling waters, with the wind shrieking round them, and a weird blue phosphoric light making everything visible, the phantom host drew nearer and nearer to the boat. But Yoshitsune did not seem to be in the least alarmed. As dauntless as ever, he stood up in the prow and faced the ghosts of the men whom he had slain in that terrible battle, and flashing forth his keen blade, said: "So you are the spirits of the Taira clan, are you? And you have risen from the ocean-bed to haunt us, and to impede our progress, and to inflict evil upon us? Have you forgotten how I drove you before me as dust before the wind when you were alive? It is a pity you have not profited by past experiences! I should have thought that you would have had no wish to see me again!"

With these words he was about to brandish his sword and attack the spectres, but Benkei, the wise and faithful Benkei, stepped up to his young master and stayed his hand, saying: "Not so, my Lord. Swords are useless against ghosts. It is not wise to anger these poor earth-bound phantoms. The best way of dealing with them is to pacify them, so that they may find peace and go to their own place."

Yoshitsune yielded to Benkei and allowed himself to be put aside. Then Benkei, who, you will remember, had formerly been a Buddhist priest, drew out a small rosary which he always carried with him, and telling his beads, and rubbing his hands together, palm to palm, began to recite prayers

They encounter the spectre army and the ghost of Taira Tomomori

earnestly and reverently in a loud voice. The sacred words appointed by the Buddhist church fell like a benediction upon the angry spirits, the wailing and the howling and the tumult of the phantom conflict ceased, and the wraiths gradually vanished into the sea from where they had arisen. Finally, the storm ceased, and the weather cleared and became as fine and peaceful as it was before, and the travellers soon reached the land in safety.

The Barrier

Across the mountains Yoshitsune now fled, and after endless adventures and hairbreadth escapes, he determined to seek the help of his old friend and partisan, general Fujiwara Hidehira, in the province of Oshu.

On the way thither they came to a guard-house at Ataka, in Kaga province. This guard-house was one of the principal frontier stations at which in those feudal times all travellers had to give an account of themselves. Yoritomo had by this time issued a proclamation ordering the arrest of Yoshitsune, so the young general and Benkei and the handful of faithful men still left to him disguised themselves as wandering priests, wearing loose caps on their heads, carrying wallets on their backs, and grasping pilgrim staves in their hands. Yoshitsune himself was disguised as a *goriki*, a servant, attendant on the priests. They travelled slowly until they came to the barrier, consulting together as to how they should pass it, for they heard that the sentries suspected everyone and were examining passers-by very strictly. Only the previous day three mendicants had been killed, owing to the suspicion of the guards having been excited.

All Yoshitsune's followers, among whom were many brave, loyal, though headstrong young fellows, wanted to storm the guard-house and cut their way through the warriors, but Benkei was strongly opposed to this and said: "No, no, that will never do! A quarrel would cost some of our lives, and we have few enough as it is. Leave the matter to me to manage and I'll get you through."

No one ever gainsaid Benkei, when he spoke with authority like that, for they all knew what a mountain of strength and resource he was in time of need. So Benkei, as ever, had his way. He disguised Yoshitsune in the dress of a *goriki*, and gave him a deep broad-brimmed hat of bamboo to wear, and made him tuck up his robe into his belt. Then, advancing in front of the others, he leisurely approached the guard-house, and with an air of the utmost unconcern and nonchalance said: "We are mendicant priests who are travelling throughout the various provinces for the purpose of soliciting subscriptions for the rebuilding of the shrine of the Great Buddha at the Tōdai temple, in Nara. We ask permission to pass the barrier."

The captain of the guard was a very clever man and a strict observer of rules, and he would not let Benkei pass without questioning him thoroughly.

"Well, as you say you are visiting the various provinces soliciting subscriptions for the purpose of rebuilding the shrine of the Great Buddha. It is possible that I may allow you to pass, but you must show me positive proof of the truth of your story," said the captain of the guard.

Benkei was staggered for a moment when he heard these words. What should he do? But he was a quick-witted man, and without betraying any sign of being taken by surprise, he answered with composure: "Very good, then, I will read you my commission written by the high priest himself in the first pages of the subscription-book."

With these words, speculating upon the ignorance of the guard, with great dignity he drew out a scroll, and pressing it with reverence to his forehead, began to improvise and read out an imaginary letter from the high priest of the Tōdai temple for the rebuilding of a shrine for the Daibutsu, at Nara. At the first mention of the name of the priest, so famous and so highly revered throughout the country, the captain of the guard fell respectfully upon his knees and listened, face bent to the earth in humble awe, to the contents of the letter. So well did Benkei play his part that the sentry was convinced of the genuine character of the commission and said: "I am satisfied. There is no reason to detain you. You may pass!"

Benkei was overjoyed, and thought that at length all difficulties had been overcome. At the head of the fugitive band, with Yoshitsune disguised as an attendant in the rear, he was moving forward to pass through the barrier when the captain suddenly darted forward and stopped Yoshitsune, saying in a loud voice: "Wait a moment, you coolie! Wait a moment!"

"We are discovered," thought Benkei. And even he, dauntless and cool in the face of all danger hitherto, felt his heart beating violently in the intense excitement of this momentous crisis.

But it was no time for hesitation, and recognizing that the whole situation hung upon that very moment, Benkei, with his usual pluck and daring, pulled himself together and coolly asked: "Have you anything to say to this coolie whom you have stopped?"

"Of course I have, and that is why I have stopped him," replied the sentry.

"And may I ask what your business with him is?" inquired Benkei.

"This coolie," answered the captain, "is said by my warriors to resemble lord Yoshitsune, and I stopped him so that I might examine him."

"What!" shouted Benkei, pretending to be overcome with laughter at the idea, "this coolie resembles Lord Yoshitsune? Ha! ha! ha! Oh, this is indeed too comical for anything! I wondered why you arrested him, but never thought of his being stopped for such an absurd reason. But as a matter of fact he has been mistaken for Lord Yoshitsune over and over again by several people, and you are by no means the only one who has had his suspicions aroused. You see the fellow is handsome and has a very white skin like an aristocrat, and that's all the good there is about him, but on that account I have had an immense amount of trouble with him."

Then Benkei turned to Yoshitsune, saying: "Wretched creature! it is all your fault that we come under suspicion all the time. You shuffle along in such a cowardly manner and put on such strange airs that people naturally suspect you. In future be more careful, and walk along like a man and not in such a mincing way, you fool!"

Thus Benkei feigned to lose his temper, and after scolding Yoshitsune roughly, finally lifted his staff and gave him several blows across the back, telling him to fall upon his knees and not presume to remain standing in the presence of the guard.

The captain of the guard had been watching this scene for some moments, and when he saw Benkei start in and thrash Yoshitsune, his doubts were completely allayed. He thought that if the apparent servant were really Yoshitsune and the mendicant priest the latter's retainer, the vassal would never dare to assault his master in this fashion.

"Ah! it was my fault and carelessness. Evidently it was an entire mistake on our part to think this coolie was Lord Yoshitsune, and it is not the poor fellow's fault, so pray do not beat him any more! Continue your journey at once and take him with you."

Benkei's trick thus succeeded completely. The captain reentered the guard-house and the young lord and his vassals passed at last unhindered through the strictly guarded gate, saved as ever by the quick-wittedness of Benkei.

Now some say that the captain of the guard was not deceived; that he knew that the disguised priests and attendant were Yoshitsune and his party, but his whole sympathy was with the hunted hero and his brave few and he allowed them to pass. For a samurai must ever show mercy and sympathy, especially to his fellows and to those in distress. The strict examination he insisted upon was a farce he played to satisfy the authorities at Kamakura.

Yoshitsune and his followers were filled with admiration at the wisdom of Benkei, and great were the praise and thanks they rendered him on this occasion. But Benkei, full of reverence and devotion to his master, never ceased to deplore the necessity which drove him to beat his own lord and apologized with great humility. Whenever the story was told, he would shed tears of sorrow and declare that he would rather have been beaten to death himself than have been obliged by circumstances to strike Yoshitsune.

Thus once by force of arms he put to flight the would-be assassins of Yoshitsune at Kyoto. By reciting Buddhist prayers he had laid to rest the ghosts of the Taira warriors in the sea at Dan no Ura. By sheer wit and sagacity he had brought his party across the dangerous frontier. And at length he managed to arrive safely with his beloved master at the Oshu residence of the famous general Hidehira.

He now thought that all troubles were over. But unfortunately this story soon reached Kamakura, and Yoritomo, furious at Yoshitsune's daring, despatched a large army to chastise him.

At this time Yoshitsune's camp was pitched beside the Koromo River, and the army from Kamakura, swarming up in countless thousands on the opposite bank, discharged volley after volley of arrows at the brave but ill-fated band. Yoshitsune's handful of men were entirely unable to face the overwhelming numbers, and fled in confusion, seeking shelter in the neighboring woods and valleys or hiding themselves in the mountains. But Benkei, despising flight, refused to budge, and stood without moving while showers of arrows fell like rain around him. At length the enemy saw that Benkei stood immovable with his seven weapons on his back, grasping his great halberd in both hands. Wondering at the sight, they drew near for the purpose of solving the mystery. As they approached, the giant still remained standing. Not an eyelid flinched, as his eyes, wide open, glared fiercely at the warriors. No wonder that the giant did not stir, for arrows were sticking all over his body like quills on a porcupine, and it was evident that he had died standing with his face to the enemy.

HÔJÔ TOKIYORI

The Hospitable Samurai

Long, long ago, in the reign of Emperor Go-Fukakusa, there lived a famous regent of the name of Hōjō Saimyōji Tokiyori. Of all the Hōjō regents he was the wisest and justest, and was known far and wide among the people for his deeds of mercy. At the age of thirty, Tokiyori resigned the regency in favor of his son Tokimune, who was only six years old. He then retired to a monastery for several years. Sometimes stories reached his ears of the miscarriage of justice, of the cruelty of the officials under him, and of the suffering of the peasants, and he determined to find out for himself if all these things were true. It was the desire of his life to see the people governed wisely and justly and impartially, to deal reward and punishment fairly alike to the rich and the poor, to the great and the lowly. After much thought he decided that the best way to achieve his end would be to find out for himself the condition of the people, so he determined that he would disguise himself and travel about amongst them unknown. He had it given out that he was dead, and had a mock funeral performed with all the pomp and ceremony due to his exalted rank. He then left Kamakura disguised as a travelling priest unknown to any one.

After journeying from place to place, he came one day to Sano, in the province of Kōzuke. It was in the depth of winter, and on this day he found himself overtaken by a heavy snowstorm. There were no houses near.

120

Tokiyori then ascended a hill, but even from that height, search as he might, he could see no sign of any dwelling, near or far. Confused and lost, he wandered about for hours. The darkness began to fall when he found himself in a hilly district. Tired and hungry, he resigned himself to passing the night under the shelter of a tree, when suddenly he spied in the distance the brown line of a thatch-roofed cottage breaking the white slope at the foot of the nearest hill. He made his way quickly towards it and knocked at the closed storm-doors.

Tokiyori heard someone move within and then come to the porch. The storm-shutter was pushed aside and a beautiful woman looked out.

"I have lost my way in the storm, and know not what to do! Will you be so kind as to give me the shelter of your roof this night?" said Tokiyori.

The woman scanned the traveller from head to foot. Then she said: "I am very sorry for you. I would willingly give you shelter, but my husband being absent I cannot let you in. You had better go on to the next village of Yamamoto, which is very near, and there you will find a good inn and accommodation for travellers!"

"You are right," answered Tokiyori. "But alas! I am so tired that I can walk no more. For pity's sake, let me sleep on the verandah or in your storehouse; for so much shelter I shall be grateful."

"I am indeed sorry to refuse you," answered the woman. "But in the absence of my husband I cannot give shelter to a strange traveller. Were he at home, he would with pleasure take you in and give you lodging for the night. Try to make your way to the next village."

Tokiyori, greatly impressed by her virtuous and modest behavior, bowed and said as he took his leave: "There is no help for it! I must try to reach Yamamoto, since you cannot shelter me to-night."

So the ex-regent of Kamakura, spent and cold and hungry, turned once more to meet the inclement weather. He took the direction pointed out to him and plodded on through the snow. But alas! the storm had increased in violence, and the snow fell faster and faster, and the wind howled across the white drifts, whirling clouds of snow in his face till at last he found it impossible to go on. He stood still in the storm, not knowing what to do. Exerting all his strength, he found it difficult to put one foot before the other. Just as he began to give himself up for lost, he heard a voice calling him from behind.

"Stop! stop!" at first faintly, then gradually the cries grew nearer and more distinct.

Wondering who else could be out in such merciless weather, Tokiyori turned in the direction where the cries came and saw a man beckoning to him to turn back.

"Are you calling me?" asked Tokiyori.

"Yes indeed," replied the man. "I am the husband of the woman who turned you away from that cottage just now. I regret that I was not at home to offer you the poor hospitality that is all I have to give. Please turn back with me. I can at least give you shelter for the night, though my house is only a small hut. You will be frozen to death if you go on in this storm."

The priest rejoiced when he heard these kind words, and as he turned back with his host he uttered many words of thanks. When they entered the porch, the woman whom he had already seen came forward and welcomed the stranger cordially, apologizing for her former behavior.

"I pray you pardon me," she said, bowing to the ground, "for my rude words a short time ago. But now that my husband has returned I hope you will pass the night under our humble roof. I beg you not to be angry with me, knowing the custom of these times."

"Don't mention it, my good woman," replied the priest in disguise. "It was quite right of you to refuse me admittance in your husband's absence. I admire your prudent conduct."

While the priest and the hostess were thus exchanging civilities, her husband had entered the little sitting-room and arranged some cotton cushions on the mat. Having done this, he came out to usher in the guest.

"Thank you," answered the priest, taking off his snow-covered hat and rain-coat. And, slipping his feet out of the sandals, he entered the house.

The host turned again to his guest and said: "Now, as you see, I am a very poor man and I cannot give you a good dinner such as the rich can offer, but to our coarse, simple fare, such as it is, you are very welcome."

The priest bowed to the ground and said that he would be grateful for any food that would stay his hunger. He had walked all day in the cold and had eaten nothing since breaking his fast in the early morning.

Meanwhile the wife busied herself in the kitchen, and as it was now the hour of sunset, the meal was soon ready to be served. The priest noticed that millet instead of rice filled the bowls, and that there was not a sign of fish in the soup, which was made of vegetables only. The disguised ex-regent had never eaten such coarse food in his life before, for millet is the poorest peasant's fare. But "Hunger needs no sauce," says the proverb, and so Tokiyori was surprised to find with how great a relish he could eat what was set before him, for he was ravenously hungry. Never had food tasted so sweet to him before. He long remembered the sensation of pleasant surprise as he partook of the first mouthful. The good wife waited on them during the meal, according to Japanese custom.

When supper was over, they all sat round the hearth, talking of the good old times and telling each other amusing stories to while away the time. The hours flew quickly by and it was midnight before the host and his guest knew it. The fire had burned very low without their noticing it, and they began to shiver with cold. The host turned to the fuel-box, but all the charcoal and wood had been burned up. Then the host arose, and, regardless of the falling snow and the bitter cold, went into the garden and brought thence three

The priest (right) is warmly received by Sano Genzaemon and his wife

125

pots of *bonsai* trees, for the training of which Japanese gardeners are famous all the world over.

"On such a winter's night a good fire is necessary for the entertainment of a traveller, but, alas! all the charcoal has been used up and I have no more in the house. To warm you before you retire I will therefore bum these trees!"

"What!" said the astonished guest, for he saw that the trees were of no common kind, but were of some value, for they were old, and their training showed the skill of an experienced gardener. "These pine, plum, and cherry trees are too good to be used as fuel—they are finely trained. No! no! you mustn't burn them for me—they are far too valuable!"

"Don't trouble yourself," said the host. "I loved them once when I was rich and had many more such valuable trees in my possession. But now that I am ruined and living in this miserable condition, of what use are such trees to me, pray tell me?" and with these words he began to break up the trees and to put the pieces on the fire. "If they could speak, I am sure they would say how pleased they were to be used for such a good purpose as your comfort!"

The disguised ex-regent smiled as he watched the kind man break up his pet trees, and make up the fire. Since Tokiyori had first entered the house, small and poverty-stricken though it was, he had felt that his host was no common farmer as he pretended to be. He felt that he must be a man in reduced circumstances.

"I feel sure," said the priest, "that you are no farmer by birth. Indeed in you I recognize the a courtesy and breeding of a samurai. Will you add one more favor to the rest you have shown me this night and tell me your real name?"

"Alas," answered the farmer in disguise, "I cannot do so without shame."

"Do not trifle with me," said the priest, "for I am very much in earnest. Tell me who you are. I should very much like to know."

Pressed so earnestly to reveal himself, the host could no longer refuse.

"Since you wish so earnestly to know, I will tell who I am, without reserve," he answered. "I am no farmer, as you rightly guessed. I am in reality a samurai, and my name is Sano Genzaemon Tsuneyo."

"Indeed? Are you Sano Genzaemon Tsuneyo? I have heard of you. You are a samurai of high rank, I know. But tell me, how is it that you are now in such reduced circumstances?"

"Oh, that is a long story," replied Sano. "It was through the dishonesty of an unworthy relation. He seized my property, little by little, without my knowing it, and one day I found that he had taken everything and that I was left with nothing except this farmhouse and the land on which it stands."

"I am sorry for you," said Tokiyori. "But why haven't you brought a lawsuit against your relation? I am sure you would recover your lost property."

"Oh yes, I have thought of that," said the farmer. "But now that Tokiyori, the just regent, has died, and as Tokimune his successor is very young, I felt that it was useless to present my petition, so that I determined to resign myself to poverty. But though I live and work like a farmer, in heart and soul I am still a samurai. Should war break out or even a call to arms be sounded, I shall be the first to go to Kamakura, wearing my armour, dilapidated and torn though it may be, carrying my halberd, rusty as it is, and riding my old horse, emaciated and unpresentable though he is, and I will do glorious deeds once more and die a warrior's death. I never for one moment forget my ambition. This alone buoys me up through all my trouble and poverty," he added cheerfully, looking up at his listener with a smile.

"Your purpose is a good one, and worthy of a true samurai," said the priest, and he smiled and looked at the warrior intently. "I prophesy that you will rise in life in the near future, and I feel sure that I shall see you and congratulate you at Kamakura on obtaining your heart's desire."

While they were talking, the night had passed and day began to break. The snow had ceased to fall, and as Sano and his guest rose to open the storm-doors, the sun rose bright and shining on a silvered world.

The priest went to put on his rain-coat and hat.

"Thank you," he said, "for all the kindness and hospitality you have shown me. I will say good-bye. Now that the storm has ceased, I need trespass no longer on your goodness. I will be getting on my way!"

"Oh," said the warrior, "why need you hurry so? At least stay one more day with us, for you seem to me no longer a stranger but a friend, and I am loth to see you depart."

"Thank you," replied the priest, "but I must hurry on. I take my leave with the firm conviction that fate will give us the pleasure of meeting again ere long. Remember my words. Good-bye!" And thus speaking, with several bows the priest turned from the porch and wended his way through the snow.

When he had gone the warrior remembered that he had forgotten to ask the traveller's name, so he and his wife would probably never know who the sympathetic stranger was.

The next spring the bakufu at Kamakura issued a proclamation calling upon all warriors to present themselves in battle-array before the regent. When Sano Genzaemon heard of this, he thought that some extraordinary event must have taken place. What it was he could not imagine. But he was a warrior and must answer the summons promptly. Here might be the chance of proving his warriorly prowess, for which he had been waiting so long, hidden away in obscurity and the poverty of his circumstances. The only thing that weighed him down was the thought that he had no money either to buy a new suit of armour or a good horse. No hesitation showed itself in the despatch with which he hastened to Kamakura, clothed only in his suit of shabby armour, a rusty halberd in hand, and riding an old broken-down horse, unattended by any servant.

When Sano reached Kamakura, he found the city crowded with warriors who were riding in from all parts of the country. There were thousands of great and eminent samurai clothed from head to foot in beautiful armour, their suits, their helmets, and their swords glittering with ornamentation of silver and gold. It was a goodly sight that the sun shone on that day, framed by the great pine trees against the background of the glimmering sea beyond. The pride of life and race were there, the hauteur of birth and rank, the glory and parade of war, the glinting of helmet and clanking of steel—every warrior's armour was composed of fine metal scales woven and held together by silken threads of ruby, emerald, scarlet, sapphire, and gold. Each warrior wore his favorite color, and as the ranks moved into the sunlight or fell into the shade the whole formed an army of moving splendor, the brilliant and variegated coloring of which was like a river of rich and magnificent brocade.

As Sano, clothed in his shabby armour and riding his broken-down horse, rode in amongst the bright phalanx of warriors, how they all jeered and scoffed at him and his horse! But Sano cared little for their scorn, the consciousness that he was a samurai as good as most of them bore him up, and he laughed to himself at their pride and swagger.

"These men wear fine armour, it is true," he said to himself, "but they have lost the true samurai spirit. Their hearts are corrupt or they would not glory so in appearance. And though my armour cannot compare with theirs, yet in loyalty I can never be outdone, even by them, braggers though they be."

As these thoughts passed through his mind, Sano saw a herald approaching the gay concourse of warriors. He rode a richly caparisoned horse, and he held aloft a banner bearing the house-crest of the regent. The warriors, their armour and their swords clanging as they moved, parted to the right and left, leaving a road for him to pass. As he rode up their lines he called aloud: "The regent summons to his presence the warrior who wears the shabbiest armour and who rides the most broken-down horse!"

When Sano heard these words he thought:

"There is no warrior here but myself clothed in old armour. Alas! the governor will reprimand it me for daring to appear in such a state. It can't be helped. Come what will, I obey the summons—such is my duty!"

So with a sinking heart Sano, the dilapidated warrior, followed the herald to the governor's house. Here the messenger announced that the warrior Sano Genzaemon had come in answer to the proclamation summoning the poorest-clothed warrior to the regent.

"I am the poorest warrior here, so the required man can be none other than myself," said Sano, as he bowed low to the retainers who came out to receive him at the porch.

Sano was then ushered along endless corridors and through spacious rooms. At last the ushering officer knelt on the polished wood outside a large room, and, pushing back the white paper screen, told him to enter. The warrior found himself in the presence of the handsome young general Tokimune. On his head he wore a helmet with golden horns and the small plates of his armour were woven together with silken threads of scarlet.

The young general bowed to the warrior in answer to his prostrations and said: "Are you the warrior Sano Genzaemon Tsuneyo?"

"Yes, I am he," answered Sano.

"Then," answered the young man, "I have to present you to someone!" and he made a sign to an attendant.

Upon this the servant pushed open the screens of an inner room, and the regent Saimyōji Tokiyori, who had been reported dead for a year, was revealed, magnificently dressed in his robes of office. Over his armour he wore a sacerdotal robe of rich brocade, and on his head a white head-dress.

Bewildered by all the strange things that were happening to him, and fearful of he knew not what, the warrior had kept his face to the ground. He heard the rattle of armour and the swish of heavy silk moving towards him over the mats, and he wondered if it were not all a dream.

Then a voice said: "Oh, Sano Genzaemon—is it you? It is long since I saw you! Look up! Don't be afraid! Don't you know me?"

The poor warrior knew at once that he had heard that voice before, and at last found courage to raise his head and to look at the resplendent figure that addressed him.

An exclamation of surprise burst from the lips of Sano, for he recognized in the personage who addressed him the priest whom he had sheltered on the night of the great snowstorm a year agone.

"You are surely," said Sano after a pause, "the travelling priest who passed that night of the great snowstorm under my roof last year, are you not?"

"Yes, I am that priest, and also I am the regent Saimyōji Tokiyori."

"Oh!" exclaimed Sano, bowing to the ground, "pardon my rudeness to you that night, for I did not know who my august visitor was," and his heart filled with fear at the remembrance of his unceremonious behavior on that occasion.

Then the ex-regent spoke again, and this time solemnly: "Sir Sano, you have no need to apologize, far from it. Do you remember what you said to me that night when the snowstorm took me to your house? You told me that through unfortunate circumstances you were now obliged to work like a farmer, yet if ever the occasion arose that should sound the call of warriors to arms, you would, regardless of your shabby accoutrements, answer the summons and come forth in the spirit of a samurai to do glorious deeds worthy of your sword once more before you died! Herewith I give you back the thirty villages in the district of Sano, of which you were robbed by your unworthy kinsman. And do you think I have forgotten your kind action when you burned your precious trees, the last relics of your prosperous past, to minister to my comfort during that terrible storm? The glow of that fire remains in my heart to this day. By way of expressing my thanks for your hospitality that cold and dreary night, in return for the pine tree (*matsu*), I am going to give you the village of Matsuida, in the province of Kōzuke. In the place of the plum tree (*ume*), the village of Umeda, in the province of Kaga. And in return for the cherry tree (*sakura*), you shall have Sakurai, a village in the province of Etchū."

As the warrior listened to these golden words of fortune, which dropped like jewels from the mouth of the beneficent regent, it seemed to him as if he must be dreaming, it was all so unexpected. He could not speak, for the tears rose to his eyes, and sobs of joy choked his utterance. When at last he looked up, he was alone. He made his way out of the mansion as in a trance, oblivious of all around him. The news of his promotion and of the favor he enjoyed in the estimation of the regent had already spread outside, and the men who had laughed and jeered at him before now smiled graciously and bowed respectfully as he passed along the ranks.

So Sano Genzaemon returned to Kōzuke, not as a poor farmer, but as a lord under the special favor of the regent, having won the esteem of all his countrymen by his warriorly conduct in adversity.

All rejoiced that faithfulness, honesty, and kindness had received their just reward, and none more than the good regent Tokiyori.

GLOSSARY

bonsai:	Japanese art form of growing dwarf trees in pots.
daimyō:	Feudal lord.
genpuku:	Coming of age ceremony.
geta:	Wooden clog.
goriki:	Servant.
hakama:	Trousered skirt.
harakiri:	Ritual suicide.
hibachi:	Brazier.
hototogisu:	Cuckoo.
kumo:	Spider.
matsu:	Pine tree.
mikoshi:	Sacred palanquin
sakura:	Cherry tree.
shōgun:	Hereditary military ruler during Japan's feudal era.
tengu:	A fictional red-faced creatures with long noses and bird-like wings with which it can fly.
tennin:	Maidens of heaven.
tessen:	A fighter's battle fan made of metal and used as a weapon.
ume:	Plum tree.

TOYO Press publishes books that contribute to a deeper understanding of Asian cultures. Editorial supervision: William de Lange. Book and cover design: Chōkei Studios. Printing and binding: IngramSpark. The typefaces used are Purloin, Futurist, Herculanum, and Prescript.